IN HIS BLOO[...]
"Brilliantly probe[...]
beneath the surf[...]
    —Quentin Reynolds

THE GIRL IN 304
"Setting, characterization excellent; pace good; large plus mark."
    —*The Saturday Review*

THE ACCUSED
"Daniels is a terrific writer who effortlessly captures the thoughts and feelings of the characters. In this book, which is told alternately in expository fashion and through a trial transcript, the reader comes to understand how the accused, a good decent man could have come to the point of killing his wife."
    —Dave Wilde

THE SNATCH
"Excellent characters..."
    —*GoodReads*

Harold R. Daniels Bibliography
(1919-1980)

In His Blood (Dell, 1955)
The Girl in 304 (Dell, 1956)
The Accused (Dell, 1958)
The Snatch (Dell, 1958)
For the Asking (Fawcett, 1962)
The House on Greenapple Road
  (Random House, 1966; Dell, 1969)

The Girl in 304
Harold R. Daniels

Introduction by
George Kelley

Black Gat Books • Eureka California

THE GIRL IN 304

Published by Black Gat Books
A division of Stark House Press
1315 H Street
Eureka, CA 95501, USA
griffinskye3@sbcglobal.net
www.starkhousepress.com

THE GIRL IN 304
Published by Dell Publishing Company, Inc., New York, and
copyright © 1956 by Harold R. Daniels.

"The Crime Novels of Harold R. Daniels" copyright © 1979 by
George Kelley; slightly revised from *The Mystery Fancier,* Vol.
3, No. 4, July/Aug 1979, reprinted by permission of the author.

ISBN: 979-8-88601-001-5

Cover design by Jeff Vorzimmer, ¡caliente!design, Austin, Texas
Text design by Mark Shepard, shepgraphics.com
Proofreading by Bill Kelly

First Stark House Press/Black Gat Edition: October 2022

The Crime Novels of Harold R. Daniels

by George Kelley

Harold R. Daniels was nominated for an Edgar in 1955 for his first novel, *In His Blood*. His other five novels feature the excellence of his first: interesting plots and situations, solid characterizations, and a sense of realism few crime novels achieve.

In His Blood (Dell, 1955) is the story of Milton Raskob, a worker at Hammersmith Chemical, a loner. Then something happens to change his dull, meaningless life:

> The knife was as familiar to his hand and as innocuous as a pencil, in spite of its razor edge. And yet earlier in the day he had closed his hand on the sharp edge and noticed with surprise that the steel had sliced painfully, if not seriously into his palm.
>
> There had been a flow of blood, which he rinsed off in the sink, and afterwards when he again picked up the knife to strip the mill, it felt different to him, almost like a personal possession, and he found himself gripping the wooden handle with a new and strangely pleasant familiarity. (pages 5-6)

Raskob is seized by the urge to kill, and he does. After following a school girl after a movie, he uses his knife to butcher her. The buildup to the scene is powerful and realistic.

Lieutenant Ed Tanager of Homicide is given the case. Tanager has personal problems: his daughter is hospitalized with suspected polio; Tanager's wife is an emotional zombie as a result.

Raskob endures various humiliations, and after each he feels the urge to use his knife. He almost murders a little black girl, but she gets away. Later, he butchers a small boy in the park. Finally, the fever takes over and he slits the throat of a newborn baby in its crib.

The investigation is believable, realistic, and professional as Tanager and his men hunt for the killer. The reader feels the frustration of the lack of clues; but he also feels for Raskob as a man driven beyond his limits.

In His Blood isn't a perfect book. Daniel's writing style has its weaknesses, and the dialogue wanders into clichés too frequently. But *In His Blood* is a superb study of a modern day Ripper.

Daniels' second book, *The Girl in 304* (Dell, 1956), begins with the body of a young woman found in the woods: stripped and stabbed to death. For a moment I thought Daniels was going to tell the same story as *In His Blood*, only this time from the perspective of a Georgia sheriff, Ed Masters.

But this time we aren't dealing with a psychopath: there's motive and deception involved here. The plotting is tight and the characters are more fully developed than those of *In His Blood*.

I liked *The Girl in 304* because Masters must first learn the secrets of the dead woman before he can find the killer, and in that process we discover truths about Masters and ourselves.

With *The Accused* (Dell, 1958), Daniels attempts something new. The format is radically different:

sections of testimony introduce the narrative. The evidence presented in the trial is expanded and amplified by the chapter that follows it.

Alvin Morlock is a simple man teaching at a small college. He is unexceptional. He lives a lonely, studious life. But he meets Louise Palaggi, a tramp, and in a moment of supreme foolishness marries her. From that moment he is doomed.

But Daniels is subtle enough to make Morelock's fate a tragic event by increments. Although two people are destroyed in this book, the crime is one of being punished for stupidity and pride rather than the usual premeditation. *The Accused* displays Daniels' growth in writing skill and characterizations.

With his next book, Daniels gets even better. John D. MacDonald said, "Harold Daniels' *The Snatch* belongs among the modern classics of crime and punishment." *The Snatch* (Dell, 1958) involves three men desperate enough to kidnap the grandchild of a Mafia godfather, but men who lack the toughness and professionalism to get away with it.

Mollison is a grifter who's come to the end of his road. He's working for a used car company and is caught trying to work a con on the company. Mollison needs money to avoid a prison sentence.

Mollison knows Morgan, a bank teller who wants to live as well as the wealthy side of the Morgan family lives. Morgan needs money.

Mollison also knows Patsy, a handyman of low intelligence who admires Mollison's phony style. Mollison tricks him into a part in the scheme.

The snatch comes off fine, but it's the aftermath with murder and the psychological disintegration which produces the book's finely crafted conclusion. The characters create their own doom in their own special ways.

The Snatch is Daniels' best balanced book, reflecting narrative control and tight plotting.

For the Asking (Fawcett, 1962) features a character very much like Milton Raskob, the psychopath from *In His Blood*. Lawrence Merrick is a high school English teacher. He's pushing forty. He has no close friends. He's an indifferent teacher whose students consider him boring and stupid. The administration correctly labels him as a time-server.

But when Merrick assists at a school dance, he's presented an opportunity to exercise the power and control he craves. While searching the school grounds for necking couples, Merrick stumbles on two students about to make love: Don Scott is the teen-aged son of the town's doctor, while the girl, Jean Cole, is from the poor side of town.

Merrick uses his discovery of their activity to blackmail Scott for money and Jean Cole for sex. Slowly, Merrick's power over these two young people begins the chain of events that'll destroy them all. When Jean Cole becomes pregnant, Merrick's mind bursts into a frenzy of hatred and murder.

For the Asking is a solid book. Its theme of dominance and submission painfully illustrates the ironies of youth and age.

With *House on Greenapple Road* (Random House, 1966; Dell, 1969) Daniels brings all of his experience and craftsmanship together. It is simply a stunning book, excellent in all respects.

A neighbor calls the police. Detective Dan Nalon comes out to the house on Greenapple Road. Here's how Daniels describes the community it's a part of, Fruit Hill Farms:

Fruit Hill Farms is the name of a development on the outskirts of Holburn, Massachusetts. The name is a double and very nearly a triple misnomer. The Farms are small plots, barely big enough to meet zoning requirements. There is, in the literal sense of the word, no fruit on Fruit Hill. The hill itself is an exaggerated knoll.

In the spring it is briefly attractive. The residents of many of the streets, bored with winter, break out their hoes and rakes; their spades and seed spreaders. The local supermarket does a sporadic business in Milorganite and Turf-Gro and Halts and a dozen other preparations with inspired names. For a time the grass is green and well trimmed. Tulips blossom. The real estate developer, however, cannily sold off the topsoil. The grass fades early. Most of the residents give up the battle early and revert to their winter hobbies of beerdrinking and propagation. A few die-hards bring in loam and fight on, damning their neighbors for not keeping their dandelions and crabgrass under control. (page 1)

That is good writing, capturing the tedium and futility of suburban developments with cute names.

When Nalon reaches his destination he finds a kitchen covered with blood: seven pints of it. The press converge like barracuda, calling it "The Red Kitchen Murder." However, police can't find the body. Marian Ord, the missing woman, becomes the object of a multi-state search.

But Nalon does a search of his own, and, like a time machine, uncovers Marian Ord's strange, torrid past. Daniels exposes it carefully, skillfully, in a series of flashbacks. The ski instructor, the preacher, the lifeguard, the motorcycle fan, the salesman, the bookie. The path of Marian Ord's life is like a minefield.

Nalon follows the case to the surprising conclusion

and the result is perhaps Daniels' best book. I highly recommend *House on Greenapple Road* and the rest of Daniels' novels. He's a fine writer and his books will give you hours of suspense and enjoyment.

— Reprinted from *The Mystery Fancier*, Vol. 3, No. 4, July/Aug 1979 (slightly revised).

The Girl in 304
Harold R. Daniels

Dedication—with thanks to Don Fine

CHAPTER ONE

A buzzard, patrolling the Georgia sky, suddenly began to spiral down in long, sweeping reaches, its descent observed by other patrolling buzzards who extended their orbits so that they could see what had attracted the first scavenger. The bird landed with a diminishing gymnastic of awkward, lurching hops, all its airborne grace taken from it, some twenty feet away from the object that had attracted it in the first place. It sidled ahead cautiously to investigate. All seemed well and it moved closer, an incredibly ugly brown bird with a wattled, naked head, which suddenly shot forward. The heat had already started to build up in the little glade. A second buzzard landed and a third began its descent.

When the boy turned off the road near the glade he saw the buzzards. Robert Hansen, called Cotton for his tow head, was on this morning a twelve-year-old Davy Crockett, hunting meat for his party of pioneers with a single-shot .22 rifle. He knew you couldn't shoot buzzards—there was a fine for killing them—but it wouldn't do any harm to sneak up on them and pretend. Bent over close to the ground with the rifle carried at the ready, he advanced, taking cover behind the young loblolly pines that bordered the glade. The buzzards were engrossed and did not see him until he was within a few feet. Then he saw the motionless human body that had attracted them, and he dropped the little rifle and ran.

Marge Hansen had known a moment of complete panic when she saw her son running toward the house. Her first thought had been that a pine rattler had struck him—nothing less would have made him drop the little gun.

Now she watched the ribbon of blacktop that was the Kingsbridge Pike. Where the straight length of road merged with the growth of scrub pine that bordered it an automobile appeared, first as a sparkling mote of glass windshield. It rapidly gained substance to become a dusty gray car that pulled up, with a squealing of rubber, before the Hansen mailbox. She recognized the car before she saw the insignia on its side, and she grudgingly conceded that the sheriff had been prompt in getting here in answer to her telephone call. A tall man, dressed in cuffless khaki trousers with a lightweight poplin jacket over a white shirt got out from the right side. He took off his light gray rancher's Stetson and bobbed his head.

"You're Mrs. Hansen?" he asked. "I'm Sheriff Masters. I'll be obliged if you'll ask the boy to show us where the—where he found it."

She sniffed. "I'll do no such thing. He's already seen more than a shirt-tail boy ought to be seeing. Reckon you can find it for yourself. It's off the road a half mile down yonder—where that tall pine sticks out."

Masters nodded. "We can find it, I guess, Mrs. Hansen. Don't blame you for not wanting the boy to go down there with us. I'll need some sort of statement from him by and by but I'll keep it simple and try not to bother you people any more than I can help."

Somewhat appeased, Marge Hansen said, "You'll be Dave Masters' boy. I'm glad you got elected. We don't get much call for sheriffs and such out here, but it's nice ..."

Cotton tugged at his mother's arm. "Ask him," he pleaded.

Marge Hansen continued: "... when the sheriff is a friend, like. And if you find the boy's rifle down there I'd be obliged if you'd drop it off on your way back."

"I'll be glad to, Mrs. Hansen," Masters said, and got back into the car.

A smallish man dressed in corduroy slacks and a sleeveless blue shirt sat at the wheel. "Where to, Ed?" he asked.

"About half a mile down the road, where that pine sticks out. Park out on the edge of the road, Tom, so Doc Adams and the others can see the car when they show up. That way they won't have to bother Mrs. Hansen."

They pulled up a hundred yards short of the pine that was their marker and got out.

"Walk up the road," Masters said. "Watch for tire marks or footprints. We probably won't be able to find much in this hard clay but there's a bare chance. I'll cut in from here."

The sheriff leaped across the ditch that bordered the road and made his way forward through the underbrush, his gray eyes alert. Moving easily and silently, he emerged into the clearing before the buzzards—there were more than a dozen of them now—were aware of his approach. In disgust and revulsion he flushed the birds. They lurched awkwardly into the air. Momentarily he watched them before he strode forward.

In three years as sheriff of Clay County Ed Masters had been concerned with death many times—too many, he felt. Not often, he thought, was it as ugly as this. His mouth twisted in an involuntary scowl of distaste and pity. The body was that of a girl. In her mid-twenties, he estimated. Her remains lay before him in a grotesque huddle, stripped nearly nude. One arm and leg were outstretched as if in approaching death she had sought to crawl away from her slayer. Dried blood had caked, masking her face and upper body. Masters turned away and called to his deputy.

"Tom," he shouted. "I've found it. Come in here but don't come straight in from the road."

The deputy came crashing through the brush, halting sharply as he saw the body. After a minute he said, "Lord, Ed! What do you think happened? Think she might have been hit by a car and thrown in here?"

Masters shook his head. "I doubt it. It's thirty feet to the road and I doubt if a car would have thrown her this far, although it's possible. But it wouldn't have torn her clothes off. Knocked her out of her shoes if it hit her but she's got hers on. Might even have torn her dress off if it was some lightweight, one-piece affair but if that happened there would be pieces of it left, and I don't see any. This is a murder. Start looking around but don't trample things any more than you can help. There might be part of that dress or a purse. We won't touch her until Doc Adams gets here."

Thirty minutes later when they heard two more cars pull up beside the road they had found nothing but the rifle that had been abandoned by Cotton Hansen.

The three men who came into the glade were headed by a man in his sixties, dressed in black serge in spite of the heat and carrying an old-fashioned medical bag. Masters greeted him. "Morning, Doc. Morning, Charlie—Jake." The man called Jake carried a Speed Graphic.

Adams said, "Mornin', Ed. This it? I'll have a look. Buzzards been at her already. Makes it tough." The coroner bent over the body and made staccato comments as he examined it. "Young woman. Maybe twenty-five. Must have been pretty once. Hard to say how long she's been dead, offhand. Lost a lot of blood before she died."

He stood up after a few minutes. "Ed, I wouldn't want to say anything you'd hold me to until I can make a detailed examination and I can't do that here—but I can tell you that this is bad trouble, not an ordinary woman-killing. She's been stabbed more than a dozen times."

"How long has she been dead?"

The coroner plucked at his lower lip. "In this heat I'd only be guessing. But for a guess, maybe ten hours or so."

Masters said, "Do what you can, Doc." To the deputies he said, "Spread out and keep looking."

The man Masters had called Charlie had taken one brief look at the body and turned away. The sheriff now looked at him. "You got word quick enough," he said. He made a question of the statement.

Charlie was young—twenty-seven or eight, perhaps. He was stockily built and carried himself very erectly as if to make the most of his height. His face was thin for his build and his eyes were green and alert-looking. He was well-dressed in a light, single-breasted suit.

"The woman who called in made her report to the police department," he said. "When they found it wasn't in their jurisdiction they referred her to you. Chief Trowbridge called the city desk about it. I called your office to find out if Jake was coming out with the coroner. When he said he was, I decided to follow him on out here instead of waiting until you got back to town."

Masters bent down to pick up the rifle, which he had leaned against a tree. "You get around more than most, Charlie," he said. "You ever see that girl before by any chance?"

Charlie shook his head. "Not that I remember, Ed. I didn't look close."

"Don't blame you. I'm going to take this rifle back to the Hansen place and call for some help. Tell Tom Danning I said he was to be in charge until I get back, will you, Charlie? Doc, I'll try to round up a coroner's jury for you while I'm gone."

The road was narrow. Masters had to back and fill several times before he got the car turned around.

At thirty-five Ed Masters looked much as he had looked at twenty and as he would look at fifty—a lean, spare man with a quietly confident bearing. He talked the idiom of his boyhood, the drawled vowels and lazy consonants of the Georgia coastal plain. He did so from choice. He had worked for an education and had put it to good use. The lazy speech and placid manner were merely an easy-going conformation with local habit.

Marge Hansen was standing in her yard when he parked the county car for the second time beside her mailbox. Masters tipped his hat. "I brought your boy's gun," he said. "If you don't mind, Mrs. Hansen, I'd like to use your telephone."

"Go right ahead, Sheriff. I've sent Cotton after his pa. He should be back any minute. Phone's in the parlor."

Masters followed her into the house and picked up the telephone, asking for a long-distance connection. He was put through almost at once. The voice at the other end of the wire said, "Georgia Bureau of Investigation. Cooper speaking."

"This is Sheriff Ed Masters from Clay County," he said. "We've got a murder on our hands down here and the way it shapes up now I'm going to need some help."

The man called Cooper asked for and was given details. When he had them he said, "Wait a minute and I'll see who we can send down." Masters heard the scrape of a chair being shoved back and the sound of receding footsteps. After several moments Cooper came back on the line. "We're sending Lieutenant Dunn down. He'll leave in an hour with the mobile laboratory. He says he knows you—worked with you on a murder case when you were a deputy."

Masters thanked him and hung up, a smile wrinkling the corners of his wide mouth. He remembered Dunn and liked him. He looked up to see Marge Hansen coming back into the room. With her was a heavy-set man in overalls and a blue chambray shirt. His face, which might ordinarily have been kindly, looked stern and hard under a two-day growth of beard.

"Sheriff Masters?" he asked, extending his hand. "I'm Rob Hansen. Marge told me what Cotton found yonder. We'll be glad to do anything we can to help."

Masters shook hands and sat down again. "That's decent of you," he said. "Most folks don't like to get mixed up in such things." He saw the boy peering around the door and called to him. "Cotton, I brought your rifle back. Your ma has it."

"Now then," he said after the boy had come in, stammered his thanks and fled in embarrassment. "You might be able to tell me if you heard any traffic on the Pike last night."

Rob Hansen frowned in thought. "There's always some traffic, Sheriff. It used to be there was a lot until they finished the Savannah cut-off. Nowadays about all we get is local traffic—people that live out this way. Most of them, though, don't travel much after sundown or a little later except Sat'day nights. Then there's trucks. When the highway department sets up a weighing station on the cut-off, some of the old timers, if they're overloaded, use the Pike. Like I said, there's always some traffic."

Masters nodded. "And there are always runners driving liquor between here and the dry counties north, I expect. I'd hoped that any really late cars going by would have stuck in your mind. We haven't fixed the time of death yet but some time last night a car must have stopped about where Cotton found that girl's body. Did you see any headlights down there, or hear anything at all unusual?"

Hansen shook his head. "I'm sorry, Sheriff. We were right here all night. I didn't see a thing. Did you, Marge?"

She looked at her husband and said thoughtfully, "Not a thing, Rob."

Masters stood up. "That's about it, then," he said, and shook hands with Hansen. "I'll be getting along. By the way, Hansen, if you could round up three or four of your neighbors and come on down there it would help us. We have to get a coroner's jury together and get a verdict. It's just a formality."

Hansen agreed and Masters went on out to the county car. Something had been said that puzzled him, something that was not in the normal order of things. Halfway back to the glade he grunted in satisfaction. "Wouldn't have said that," he mused, half aloud. Hansen had been quick to state that he had been at home all night. This would be taken for granted in a rural district where people went to bed early and visited town only on Saturdays as a rule. Masters' impression of Hansen had been favorable. Hansen had struck him as a simple, probably hard-working man. Nevertheless he decided to have Tom Danning or Jake Bowen do some checking up.

A few additional cars were parked along the road beside the glade when Masters again stopped and got out, mopping his forehead. Tom Danning, hearing the car, came out to the car followed by Charlie Hess. Danning's blue shirt was already dark with perspiration and his face was drawn and white.

"Didn't find a damn thing," he said.

Masters led the way back to the glade. "I wasn't very

hopeful," he said. "I wish you'd been able to find her purse so we could get an identification."

Charlie Hess halted at the edge of the glade. "I don't want to see any more of it, Ed. I'm going to get on back to town with what I've got. Would you make a statement for the early edition?"

"I can't say much that you don't already know, Charlie. I talked to the Bureau of Investigation. They're sending a man down—Bob Dunn—you may know of him. The Hansen youngster found a body and his mother reported it and we came on out to investigate and that's about it."

Charlie nodded. "We'll go with that then. We'll play it down until we get more details. You know how we feel at the *Inquirer*, Ed. We'll co-operate in any way we can."

Masters took out his pipe and fumbled for matches. "Appreciate it, Charlie," he said. "Call my office later on if you want. Maybe we'll know who she is by then."

The reporter nodded and left, hastening through the underbrush with short, rapid steps. Masters watched him for a moment before he turned back to the body. Someone had found an old army blanket in the back of a car and thrown it over the motionless, huddled form, concealing the fact that death had denied any dignity to its owner. Doc Adams had taken a seat on a wind-toppled loblolly. He looked tired and strained, Masters thought. His white hair was matted with sweat and his face was flushed. As Masters approached he asked, "Did you get me a jury, Ed?"

"I did. They'll get here any time now. Did you find anything more? Scars or birthmarks?"

The coroner shook his head. "Nothing, Ed. Later, maybe. I don't like what I've seen so far. Apparently it wasn't a sex crime—or if it was it wasn't consummated. The underclothing is intact and there is no sign of mutilation. I counted eight stab wounds in the chest and abdomen. Whoever killed that girl hated her beyond human understanding or else he was a maniac. Maybe both. You and two deputies will play hell trying to find the murderer in the whole of Clay County. I can name you a dozen back-country families that ought to be committed as a group."

"I'll work on the idea that it was someone that hated her, and for a good reason," Masters said. "For a start I'm going on back to town and talk with the police. I'll have Jake's pictures developed while I'm at it and I'll send Gregory's hearse out to pick up the body after you've held your inquest."

Masters, with Tom Danning driving, started back for town. The deputy sat stiffly erect behind the wheel, his face set, jaw clamped tightly. After they had covered a mile he said, "I knew her, Ed."

Startled, Masters swore. "And you didn't tell me about it back there? What's the matter with you, Tom? Who was she and what do you know about her?"

Danning kept his face straight ahead, his eyes intent on the road. "Her name was Lucy Carter. I guess you'd say she was no good."

Masters said angrily, "I wouldn't say anything at all unless I knew what I was talking about. Damn it, Tom, you know that."

Danning reddened. "She works at Benny's Drive-In. That's where I met her."

Masters, still angry, said, "We couldn't indict her for that."

Danning continued: "I guess you know about my wife and me, Ed. She left to visit her folks, couple of months ago. She ain't coming back. Anyway, after she left I sort of went off the deep end, drinking and being a damn fool. She picked me up one night, or I picked her up. I don't remember now. She came home with me. The house was a pigsty, Ed. I was more'n half hog myself about that time. She stayed three days, cleaning the house and getting my meals and getting me straightened out as well as the house. And she wouldn't take any money from me when she left."

Masters had been aware of Danning's domestic troubles and he could understand, to an extent, that it embarrassed him to admit in front of Doc Adams and Jake Bowen that he knew Lucy Carter. His own anger diminished. "Did she tell you where she came from?" he asked. "Anything about her folks or herself? We've got to find somebody to notify. More than that, we've got to find out who killed her and left her body in the brush here. Her killing may not go any farther back than Clay City. Then again it may go clear back to where she came from."

"If she did I don't remember it, Ed. The way she talked she came from upstate, maybe, or maybe Carolina. You got to remember I was in a pretty bad way those days. Drunk, most nights."

"When did you see her last?"

"To talk to her it must have been a month ago. I've seen her once or twice on the street."

"Where did she stay?"

"I don't know, Ed." Danning paused. "Ed, suppose this was to get out, then there wouldn't be any chance at all for my wife and me. I'm not ashamed of the way it was with Lucy and me but if you could keep me out of it I'd appreciate it. If you have to bring me into it you have to, but I hope you won't."

Masters reflected for a moment. Danning had done a damn fool thing but no permanent harm had been done, and he had volunteered his information as soon as he had been able to speak privately. For a moment the thought flickered across the sheriff's mind that Danning would not have dared hold back indefinitely in the face of a prospective investigation. He dismissed the thought as cynical beyond reasonableness—but it left a scar. He said, "I'll do what I can, Tom."

Danning's fingers tightened on the steering wheel. "Thanks, Ed. You won't regret it." He was as aware as Masters of the wedge that had been driven into their friendship and he was trying to overcome it. "Any other case—if it had been any other way—"

Masters said shortly, "Forget it, Tom." They made the rest of the trip to Clay City in a strained silence.

When Danning parked the car in front of the courthouse Masters said, "Check up on Rob Hansen. His son found the body. See if he's got a record and find out what kind of a reputation he's got. I think you'll find he's running liquor north but you may find something else. I think he was away from home last night and he's hiding it. Work on it from that angle."

Danning nodded and started the motor again. Masters walked a block to a photographer's studio with Jake Bowen's plates and got a promise of prints within a half hour before he returned to the courthouse and entered his small office. It was an austere room, tucked under the great staircase that faced the main entrance. When Masters walked in, the jailer who looked after the half-dozen cells in the basement was the only person there. He was in the office whenever it was necessary for Masters and his deputies to be away at the same time. He said there had been no important calls and left, leaving behind him an early edition of the *Inquirer*. Masters glanced at it. Charlie Hess, true to his promise—and probably because he had no alternative, Masters reflected—had played the story down. It was boxed in the left-hand column under a sixteen-point head.

The body of an as yet unidentified woman was

*found this morning a short distance beyond the
Mussel Creek bridge by the son of a local farmer.
The slain woman, whose age was estimated by Dr.
Clinton Adams, Clay County Coroner, at about
twenty-five, had been brutally stabbed a number of
times before her body was thrown into the weeds
and brush beside the Kingsbridge Turnpike. As this
edition of the* Inquirer *was being printed, Sheriff
Edward Masters and his Deputies Thomas
Danning and Jacob Bowen were making a
preliminary investigation. Sheriff Masters informed
an* Inquirer *reporter that the State Bureau of
Investigation was being summoned into the case.*

The crime was first made known when—

Masters put down the paper and called Gregory's
Undertaking Parlors, requesting that a hearse be sent
to pick up Lucy Carter's body. He debated eating a
sandwich and rejected the idea. Instead, he leaned
back, hands locked behind his head, his eyes half
closed. He had a strong mental image of the glade
and what it contained. He studied this image carefully,
seeking some new facet which he might have
overlooked earlier. He found none.

After he had picked up the pictures at the
photographer's studio he walked the few blocks to the
city hall, turning down the corridor that led to the
police department wing. Three men were lounging in
the room he entered. All three were large; one of them
was almost a giant. They turned expressionless faces
toward him, their eyes showing hostile wariness. The
largest man nodded in recognition but with a complete
lack of friendliness in the gesture.

Masters said, "Trucks. Kirby. Cox. Chief Trowbridge
in?"

Cox was the smallest of the group but he outweighed

Masters by thirty pounds although he was no taller
than the sheriff. He was dressed in a rumpled brown
suit and his face had a smudge of beard a day overdue
for shaving. He raised small, piggish eyes to meet
Masters' glance and nodded. "He's in," he conceded.
There was a note of truculence in his voice.

The wall of enmity that existed between the sheriff's
office and the police department in Clay City was
almost traditional. It sprang from the geographical
fact that city jurisdiction ended at the bridge that
spanned the Ocmulgee River at the east end of town.
Since the establishment of that boundary the city had
grown beyond the bridge but the county retained
authority. Masters, knowing the need in an age of fast
transportation for cooperation between the two law
enforcement agencies, had occasionally tried to breach
the wall. His overtures had been rebuffed without
exception and he had long since ceased trying to
pretend that there was any basis of friendship between
the departments.

Now he studied Cox briefly, noting the stark jaw
and sullen mouth. He had earlier come to the
conclusion that police work tended to brutalize a
certain type of man—or that it brought out a latent
brutality in that type—Cox's type. He said, "Thanks,"
sardonically and pushed open the door to Trowbridge's
office.

Walt Trowbridge sat behind his desk studying an
official-looking paper. Masters had the distinct
impression that he had picked it up hastily on his,
Masters', entrance in a deliberate attempt to appear
busier than he actually was. He was a smallish man
of about fifty with thinning hair parted over his pink
scalp in a manner calculated to cover as much of the
surface as possible. His sharp eyes glinted behind a
pair of rimless bifocal lenses. Charlie Hess had once

described him—privately—as resembling Heinrich Himmler in his appearance and in the way he operated his department. With regards to appearance, Masters had admitted, the description was apt.

Now he stood up, putting out his hand and booming in a surprisingly deep voice, "Masters! Good to see you, Sheriff. You don't get over here often enough. What's this about a body?"

Masters shook the small, moist hand and took a proffered seat. "Hate to bother you people more than I have to," he said dryly.

"No bother, Sheriff. Why, I was telling the Rotary Club only last week that we ought to have better cooperation between civic authorities."

Masters had a better than fair idea of what Walt Trowbridge had told the Rotary Club. He let it pass and took out the pictures that Jake Bowen had taken. "You can't tell much about her face, Chief, but evidently this girl is local. I thought you might be able to help me out. I've got her name—Lucy Carter—and I know she worked at Benny's. Right now that's all I do know."

Trowbridge studied the pictures. He said disdainfully, "Benny's," and pushed a button. An elderly man in uniform entered the office.

"Cole," Trowbridge said, "see if we have anything on a Lucy Carter."

Cole went out and returned after a moment with a cardboard file which he handed to Trowbridge. The chief studied it briefly and shook his head. "Not much, Sheriff. Picked up once for soliciting. We held her overnight for examination and Judge Ross let her go in the morning with a warning. She gave the Oceanus House as her place of residence. Worked as a carhop when she worked."

Masters stood up. "Thanks, Chief," he said. "Now if you can spare one of your officers for an hour or so I'd like him to go with me while I ask a few questions. George Cox would be fine."

Trowbridge frowned. "Now, I don't know. We're pretty busy here—on the other hand we want to cooperate with your office to the fullest extent possible." (Masters could almost follow his line of thought word for word. He would have been willing to bet that within two minutes after his own departure from the office Trowbridge would be on the telephone. "Just want to let you know, Charlie [or Joe—or Pete], that my office is doing everything possible to help the sheriff and his men. Of course, you know that Masters hasn't had as much experience with crimes of this type as my staff.")

He thanked Trowbridge and went out. George Cox was leaning against the wall cleaning his fingernails with a jackknife. Masters said, "George, the chief said I could borrow you for a while. I've got a car outside."

Cox grunted. "What's the matter with your own deputies?" he asked sullenly.

Masters said in a level voice, "They're busy. You coming with me or do I tell Trowbridge that you refuse?"

Cox pushed himself erect and looked at Masters, seeming to be measuring him. He licked his lower lip, growled something unintelligible and took his hat from a hook on the wall. "Hell," he said, "let's go, then."

CHAPTER TWO

By the time the two men arrived at the Oceanus House, Masters had filled Cox in on the Carter investigation. The Oceanus House was constructed in that period between the nineteenth and twentieth centuries when American architects seemed least

inspired. A squat, three-story building of pinkish brick
now decorated with neon tubing, it invited attention
to its ugliness like a dowdy old dowager bedecking
herself with diamonds. The neon signs shouted that
there was a cocktail lounge within and that room
rates started at a dollar and a half. Masters parked
the car and he and George Cox got out. The lobby
matched the exterior of the building. The floor was a
mosaic of tiny marble octagons. With the years, many
of the octagons had vanished and had never been
replaced. The sweepings and moppings of half a
century had left a grayish crust where the tiles had
been. Masters paused in the lobby. "Get the key," he
said.

Cox walked, with a heavy tread, toward the desk.
He returned in a few seconds dangling a key from his
forefinger. "Third floor," he grunted.

They took a creaking elevator to the third floor. When
they got off Cox turned left. "This way," he said. "Room
304." The two men stopped before a warped and
peeling door while Cox inserted the key into the lock.
When he swung the door open a faint smell of face
powder and cosmetics met them, riding a tide of hot,
stuffy air.

The room itself was shabby but clean. A faded rug
covered the floor, the strong threads of the warp
exposed through the nap like old bones. A brass bed
stood against one wall. On it was a green satin spread.
A bureau and a chair. Masters' eye picked up a
photograph on the bureau and he reached for it. It
was a snapshot of a family group of four. In the back
row stood an elderly man. Even in the miniature
replica in the photograph he was thin and stooped.
His face was set in stern and uncompromising lines.
Beside him stood a thin woman with harried eyes. In
the front row were a boy and a girl. The boy appeared

to be in his teens; the girl was dark-haired and smiling, young and fresh in a dress with a sailor collar. Masters studied the face intently before he put the photograph down.

Cox had taken an impatient stance just inside the door. He said now, "Hell with this, Masters. You don't need me. I'll be down in the bar when you're through."

Masters, when Cox had gone, looked into the closet. There were a dozen dresses hanging from a rack that was no more than a piece of broomstick nailed across the studding. They were, most of them, light cottons and inexpensive organdies, giving an impression in mass of schoolgirlishness. He carried them out and spread them on the bed while he searched for labels. There were few and those he did find had been issued by local, large-volume stores. He returned the dresses to the closet and carried out a half-dozen pairs of shoes—cheap pumps, patent leather slippers, and a single pair of oxfords. Their labels told him nothing. He began opening bureau drawers. The first drawer held lingerie—medium priced, he would have guessed. All of it was frilly, frivolous. To one side were nylons and these were unquestionably expensive. She would have sacrificed much, he supposed, to keep her legs looking trim. The remaining drawers held blouses and slips, neatly folded. A cheap compact with a cracked mirror. An over-the-shoulder handbag. Flashy.

Masters closed the bureau drawers and picked up the photograph again, glancing at the back to see if there was a laboratory number on it. There was none. He studied it again, struck again by the freshness of the girl's face, the youthfulness that was emphasized by the sailor collar.

The top of the bureau held cosmetics. Powder. Lipstick. A scattering of bobby pins. A comb, some of its teeth missing. A brush with a snarl of dark hair caught in its bristles.

The bathroom had been carelessly partitioned off from the rest of the room. It held little of Lucy Carter beyond a toothbrush, a half-melted bar of soap and a few odds and ends. Aspirin. A rubber syringe.

He walked back into the bedroom. It was stifling hot. A poor place, he mused, to call home. A fly buzzed wearily at a window. Masters stood stock still for a moment, caught by the futility of the ugly little room. Frivolous panties and girlish dresses and in the entire room no book, no picture. Poor empty-headed kid, he thought. Not very intelligent, probably, and perhaps immoral by ordinary standards, but not deserving to lie dead in the bushes beside a country road. It came to him that he was persistently thinking of Lucy Carter not as he had seen her earlier in the day but as she looked in the picture.

There was a knock on the door, sounding strangely loud in the brooding quiet of the room, and Masters whirled. Before he could speak a woman swung the door open and stepped into the room. She was in her late twenties, he would have guessed. Her eyes were washed-out blue beneath stringy, untended yellow hair. She had lately plucked her eyebrows. Without any cosmetic on them they gave her forehead a bald, tight-skinned appearance. She wore a cotton wrapper and battered felt house-slippers. When she saw Masters she clutched the coat more tightly about her. Her tone, when she spoke, was surprised but not greatly so. Not startled.

"Who are you?" she demanded, and in the same breath, "Where is Lucy?"

Masters said, "I'm Ed Masters, Miss. Sheriff Masters." He watched her as he said the words. She stiffened and became instantly wary. Tough wary. He continued: "It might be kind of appropriate for you to tell me who you are."

"Evelyn Parks," she said. "I live in this dump. I came in to see if Lucy had any aspirin."

He nodded his head in the direction of the bathroom. "There's some in there. I'll get it for you. You want a glass of water with it?"

"Please."

He went to the medicine cabinet to get the aspirin he had seen earlier. The little kindness where it was fairly obviously not expected might strip some of the toughness from her. And in the time he was gone she could regain her balance, her composure.

When he returned and gave her the aspirin she thanked him. He said, "No trouble, Evelyn."

She swallowed the white pill and took a quick swallow of water before she asked, a shade too casually, "What did Lucy do?"

He ignored the question, not rudely but as if he had not heard it. He asked one of his own. "Lucy was a friend of yours, I gather. How long did you know her?"

"I guess you could call her a friend of mine. She came here three months or so ago." The Parks woman caught herself and her eyes narrowed. "What do you mean she *was* a friend of mine?" she demanded.

Masters said flatly, "She's dead. We found her this morning."

The blond woman shook her head. "Poor kid," she said. "What happened? Auto wreck?"

Masters said, "Not an auto wreck, Evelyn. She was murdered."

"Lucy! How did it happen—who did it?"

"We don't know yet. You might be able to help."

Her lip curled derisively. "Sure I could," she said. "What's that radio program—Nick and Nora? Call me Nora!" Her voice dropped half an octave. "Look, Sheriff, the kid lived in the same flophouse as me. I borrowed stuff from her—aspirin—lipstick. She did the same from me. You tell me somebody killed her. All right. I'm sorry and I hope you catch him and hang him. As for helping you, what could I do? I don't want any part of it. I've got enough troubles of my own."

It was difficult to appeal to a woman like Evelyn Parks. Masters tried. "For a start, I'd like you to make a formal identification of the body. We know—at least we're nearly certain—that it's Lucy, but for the record some relative or friend of hers has got to come forward and state that it's her." He added a calculated, "It's sort of the last favor anyone can do for her."

Evelyn Parks rubbed her hands nervously against the skirt of her robe. "I guess I'll have to do it," she said.

"Thanks. You said she came here about three months ago?"

"About that long. She took a room here. Up till a couple of weeks ago she worked out at Benny's Drive-In. Car-hopping. Then she quit."

"What did she do then?"

She laughed sardonically. "What do you think she did? She hustled. That's why she quit Benny. Said she might as well get paid for it since she had to hustle either way."

"Did she ever mention her family or where she came from?"

"Not to me. She was sort of a closemouthed kid in some ways. She was pretty friendly with one of the carhops out at Benny's though. A kid by the name of Hazel. Maybe she talked to her."

Masters said, "We can check that. How soon can you get dressed?"

"Give me fifteen minutes. You want me to meet you down in the lobby?"

Masters agreed and she left the room, closing the

door behind her. The sheriff, after a final glance about the room, stepped into the hall and walked to the elevator.

Cox was not in sight in the lobby. Masters went to the registration desk. The youth on duty was about twenty-five years old. His knowing eyes were red-rimmed, drooping at the corners. His frame was slight, his posture round-shouldered. Masters said, "I'm Masters. Sheriff Masters. Detective Cox came down from Room 304 ahead of me. He forgot to leave the key with me. Did he leave it here at the desk?"

The youth nodded. "Right here, Sheriff."

"Good. I want to ask you a few questions. First of all, check the registration on Lucy Carter. I want to know when she first registered here and what she gave as her permanent address."

The clerk fumbled with the ledger for a moment, then: "April 6," he said. "Three months ago yesterday. All she gave for an address was 'City.' A lot of them do that," he added. Curiosity showed for a moment in his bloodshot eyes. "What did Lucy do?" he asked.

Masters said dryly, "She died. Didn't Cox mention it?"

The clerk shook his head. "Not him. Cox doesn't tell you things. You tell him. What happened to Lucy? Auto accident?"

Masters, remembering that Evelyn Parks had leaped to the same conclusion a few minutes before, said merely, "No," not elaborating. He was worrying a piece of information the Parks woman had given him to the effect that Lucy Carter had worked for a time at Benny's Drive-In, and he was impatient to be through with the questioning.

"You knew the girl," he said. "How well did you know her? Did she ever tell you where she actually came from?"

The clerk shrugged. "She never told me anything," he said. "She came in and registered. She kept her room rent paid up as well as any of 'em." A tinge of whining resentment crept into his voice. "I made a play for her once. I wasn't good enough for her." The whining voice became sly. "You know what she was, Sheriff. Living here in this dump." The clerk adopted a man-to-man air that was repellent to Masters. He had an impulse to put his hand on the sallow face and thrust it back from him.

The clerk continued. "The other girls—well, you know how it is. Working in the same place. They'd give a guy a tumble. Not that one."

Masters said disgustedly, "Let it go. And give me the key to her room. I'm impounding it and sequestering the room. You understand what that means?" When the clerk looked puzzled he answered his own question. "It means no one goes into that room without my written approval. Don't make any mistakes about that."

The clerk shook his head in nervous agreement. Masters half turned away before he swung back to ask, "I've got a deputy named Danning. Tom Danning. Do you know him?"

"No."

This time Masters completed his turn and walked through the lobby to the cocktail lounge. It was a garish room, painted a graying salmon pink. Half a dozen round tables were scattered around the center of the room and there was a bar across one end. George Cox stood at the bar, shoulders rounded, his shark mouth clamped on a wet cigar.

Cox looked up as Masters approached. "You through?" he grumbled.

"For the time being. I've got a friend of the Carter girl to agree to make the identification. I can get along without you if you want to get back to the city hall."

Cox shrugged. He said morosely, "I come along this far with you. I might as well go on out to the morgue. They bring the stiff in yet?"

Masters sifted through his pocket for a coin. "I'm going to call from the lobby and find out," he said. "They've had time."

Cox straightened. "Who is the friend who is going to make the identification?"

"A girl by the name of Evelyn Parks." Masters glanced idly at Cox. "You know her?"

Cox said casually, "I might have bumped into her a few times. If she lives in this dump I might have pinched her more than once."

Masters called his office from the lobby. Jake Bowen answered the call. "We've about cleaned it up, Ed," he said. "Gregory's hearse picked up the body. It's at the morgue by now. Did you get anywhere with Trowbridge?"

Masters did not mention that Tom Danning had identified Lucy Carter before the sheriff talked with the police department. He said, "We found out her name and a few things about her. Did Tom call in yet? He's out checking around about Hansen." Jake said no. Masters told the deputy where he was headed and hung up.

As Masters came out of the telephone booth Evelyn Parks was leaving the elevator. She had straightened her hair and put on make-up but there was a wary stiffness in her posture as she approached. Masters smiled easily in an effort to relieve the tension that obviously possessed her. "This won't take very long," he said. He steered her toward the bar where George Cox waited. "Detective Cox from the city police department is going with us." He had been watching her face when he said this and he saw her shoulders go back and her stride shorten. "You know him?"

She said sardonically, "Not socially," and moved on into the cocktail lounge. She was carrying her head high.

Cox came ponderously up to meet them. Before Masters could speak the detective asked brutally, "This the bag that is going to make the identification?"

Masters fought down an instant fury. "Cox," he said flatly, "this woman is doing the county a service. Keep a civil tongue and treat her with normal courtesy." Watching Evelyn Parks when Cox spoke, he had seen her flinch as if she had been slapped. For a moment she had thought of herself as respectable, but Cox had destroyed the illusion.

They made the trip to the morgue in silence, Cox being openly contemptuous of the woman and Masters preoccupied with recalling everything he knew of Benny's Drive-In and, specifically, Benny Zurich, the owner of the place. Adding it up, he decided grimly that he knew quite a bit. The Drive-In was like a thousand others between Clay City and the Florida line. A combination barbecue, juke joint, motel—hot pillow version—beer joint, and dance hall. All things to all men.

Masters knew it to be the hangout of the hot-rod set of Clay City and the surrounding country—the never-grow-up sons of well-to-do cotton farmers, lumber growers, peach raisers. Harmless, some of them. Vicious when a combination of circumstances brought it out. And about Benny Zurich's viciousness, no question at all. At any time.

Benny had served time in Reidsville for armed robbery and for mayhem. Some of the brutality had been burned out of the man by the years but Masters still considered him to be both dangerous and unpredictable. Benny knew the ropes. Masters had violently sought the revocation of his license by the county commissioners after each of a half-dozen brawls at the place, but he had been totally unsuccessful. Being realistic, Masters had decided to hold back until he could make a sure case against Zurich, one of such a nature that no man in public life could take his part. A year ago he had thought he had such a case. A waitress at the place had been badly beaten. By Benny, she claimed, in the anguish of a broken jaw and a disfigured face. Masters had brought Zurich in—and the waitress had retracted every word of her accusation and claimed instead that she had fallen out of a moving automobile.

They drew up before the morgue, a small cement bulkhead attached to the county hospital, and entered. Evelyn Parks stayed close to Masters as they clattered noisily across the cement floor. An attendant, hearing them, came hurriedly into the dim, cool room through an interior doorway. Masters greeted him. "'Lo, Billy." He had seen Art Gregory's old fashioned, high-sided hearse parked unobtrusively beside the building when he drove up. "Gregory and Doc Adams inside?"

Billy, seeing the woman with Masters, hid his rubber-gloved hands behind his back. "Sure, Ed. They been here half an hour."

"Good. This lady is going to identify her for us."

"Jeez, Ed, you can't take her in there now! Let me tell Doc and we'll fix things a little."

"All right, Billy. We'll wait."

Billy hurried away and Masters found a chair for Evelyn Parks.

Cox became expansive. "Haven't been here in some time, Masters," he said, falsely genial. He glanced covertly at Evelyn, noting the white, set face. "Last time was when we took a body out of Holcomb's Pond. Should have seen it, Masters. This guy was fat and he'd been in there maybe a week. Catfish got to him before we did."

Evelyn shivered and Masters wheeled to face Cox, his eyes narrowed and angry. "Shut up, Cox," he said.

Billy came out of the inner room. He had taken off the rubber gloves.

"Doc says it's all right now."

Doc Adams and Gregory, the undertaker, had done their best. Lucy Carter was covered with a sheet except for her face. The matted dirt and leaves had been brushed from her hair so that it lay on the narrow table in a tangled heap, a dark frame for the pale face. The eyes were closed. Doc Adams had somehow managed to relax the strained facial muscles so that the staring look of fear was gone and the girl might almost have been sleeping there.

Evelyn Parks approached slowly, her eyes averted, until she was near to the table. Then she looked down.

Masters had prepared himself for nearly any sort of reaction from Evelyn. There was almost none. She looked down at the face of the dead girl and quickly looked away again. She did not cry out or stiffen. She said in a muffled voice. "That's her. That's Lucy Carter. Now get me away from here."

Masters led the girl to the outer room and silently signaled to Billy to stay with her. With Cox he returned to the autopsy room. Doc Adams was washing his hands, cupping them and letting the water run the length of his forearms. The sheriff waited quietly until the coroner turned and reached for a towel. Then he asked, "Anything?"

The coroner shrugged. "About what I told you this morning. I'm sending some of the organs to the state pathologist but it's pretty clear that she died of internal hemorrhage. She put up one hell of a fight, though. There are marks on the throat. The way I'd reconstruct it I'd say that someone tried to strangle her and she turned out to be too strong. He—or she— had to use a knife. A small knife. Jackknife, probably. About a three-inch blade."

Masters grimaced. "Any signs of an attack?"

"You mean, was she raped? I don't know. I don't think so. This may mean something to you. She had a child. About six months ago."

Masters frowned. "You said this morning that the killer might have been a maniac in view of the way she was cut up. Have you found anything to support that theory?"

"No. Other than the savagery of the attack itself. There was no sign of a sexual aberration but that doesn't mean that it didn't exist. She went into that meadow with someone. Why she went and who she went with are your problems. Maybe that person was a deviate and maybe he got panicked when he saw what he had done—before he could consummate the crime, so to speak."

Masters filled his pipe but did not light it. "We'll have to consider that a possibility, of course. The thing that bothers me most at this moment is her dress."

Doc Adams' eyes widened in mild surprise. "What dress? All she had on was a pair of panties and a brassiere and her shoes."

"That's it. What I want to know is why. We hunted that area thoroughly, Doc, and there was no sign of a dress. I'll grant you it was a hot night but it wasn't so hot she'd go riding around the country without a dress on."

Cox, who had been listening idly, spoke for the first time in minutes. "Supposing the killer got blood on him. It would be logical for him to use the dress to wipe it off."

Masters shook his head. "I don't see it. He might

have wiped the blood from his hands on the hem of her dress. Or he might have ripped a piece of cloth from it. Not the whole dress. And he wouldn't have taken it with him if he had."

Gregory, the undertaker, a round little man with a jovial face, had joined the group. "I think you're right, Sheriff," he agreed. "I've got a theory, though. It isn't a nice thing to think about in the presence of the deceased but you know how young people are these days. Supposing they were parked by the road, petting. They might have got—carried away. She could have taken her dress off then—or he could. That way it would have been left in the car—"

Cox interrupted: "If they got carried away that much they wouldn't have stopped to walk into the brush. She wasn't any high school kid with hot pants, Gregory. She was a professional. A prostitute."

Masters reached for a match and lit his cold pipe. "We'll find out," he said placidly. "There's probably a simple explanation." He turned to Cox. "You ride back with Doc Adams, Cox. I want to talk to the Parks girl."

Evelyn Parks was much calmer when Masters headed the county car back toward Clay City. She sat beside him in the front seat remote and withdrawn.

When they were halfway back to the city he said, "That was a decent thing you did. I know it wasn't easy."

She took a cigarette from her purse and lit it before she answered: "Somebody will do it for me someday. That Carter kid, though. It's a damn shame."

Masters nodded. "When was the last time you saw her, Evelyn? It's important, so think carefully."

She inhaled a long draft of smoke. "I was thinking about that," she admitted. "You know how it is when you hear that someone you know is dead. You say, 'Why, I saw her only last night,' or something like that. Well, I didn't see her last night. Sunday is slow in our set. I saw her Saturday night at Benny's Drive-In. I was with a friend. We stopped for a beer. She was in a car with a man. I couldn't see who it was. That kid Hazel I told you about waited on them. She might know."

Masters let Evelyn Parks out of the car in front of the Oceanus House. His watch indicated two-thirty when he turned to head back toward the courthouse. He was impatient to get out to Benny's place, especially now with the lead the Parks woman had given him. Driving through the traffic he let his mind drift, trying to recall if the name Hazel associated itself with the long roll of remembered incidents in which Benny Zurich had been involved. It did not.

CHAPTER THREE

Tom Danning and Jake Bowen were both in the office when Masters entered, tossed his hat on the desk and sat down. Bowen said, "Charlie Hess called a while back. He got the girl's name from Trowbridge so he said he wouldn't bother you at the morgue. Said he'd be over to see you after a while."

Masters grunted. Charlie Hess, he was aware, played the police department against his, Masters', office when it suited his own purpose. And Charlie Hess had only one purpose. To get ahead, in the old-fashioned phraseology. With the grunt he dismissed Hess. "Did you hear from Lieutenant Dunn yet?" he asked.

Bowen shook his head. "Don't see how he could get here for a good half hour yet."

Masters turned to Tom Danning. "What about Hansen?"

"I checked around at the bank and a few other places," Danning said. "He bought the farm out across the creek five years ago. Two years ago there was an early frost—you remember that, Ed. It pretty near ruined him. He's been doing a little liquor running north to the dry counties to get cash money."

Masters grinned. "Bank tell you that?"

Danning smiled. "Not in so many words. No, I just checked at the package store to see how much he's been buying. About that, Ed—he ain't doing anything that a number of people I could name aren't doing. Far as I can make out, Hansen is a pretty square, reliable man. Give him time and a crop and he'll be all right. You want me to do anything more about him?"

Masters, after a moment's thought, said, "Yes. Go on out there and face him with what you know. From the evasive way he acted with me I'd be willing to make a small bet he made a trip north Sunday night. Let him know that we know about the liquor hauling but that we don't plan to take any action on it if he cooperates. Get a little tough with him if you have to—but I don't think you will. If he heard or saw anything Sunday night I want to know what it was."

Danning stood up. "All right, Ed. Anything else?"

"One thing. Pick up a couple boxes of .22 shells and take 'em out to the boy."

Bowen said, as Danning left, "What about me, Ed?"

"I'm going out to Benny's Drive-In. You hold down the office until I get back."

Benny's Drive-In was two miles out of town; a sprawling collection of buildings. Glass brick and neon in the front and a row of tiny, jerry-built cabins in the back, reminding Masters of a line of privies. He found no humor in the thought as he swung the car into the blacktop parking area. There were two carhops on duty, dressed alike in cowboy boots of white leather that made their legs look slim and girlish, the briefest of shorts and flimsy halters that emphasized their round breasts.

One of the carhops came up to the car, apparently not noticing the sheriff's department insignia on the side of the door. Close up she was not as girlish as she had seemed at first glance. Her face was hard, her voice nasal and whining as she asked for his order.

"Is Hazel on duty?" Masters asked.

"Hazel King? Yair. You want her?"

"Please."

The girl turned and went off to speak to the second girl. Watching, Masters saw Hazel glance toward his car, hesitate and then come toward him. She was younger than the first girl. Hardly twenty, he decided. Her dark hair was loose around her face, caught above the forehead with a narrow piece of yellow ribbon. Her eyes were as dark as her hair; wide eyes, set a shade too close for genuine beauty. Smallish nose; a full mouth with a short upper lip. A round figure, verging on the plump side, with smallish breasts and full hips.

Masters introduced himself, using his title, which was unnecessary. He had caught her quick glance at the insignia on the car. With the glance there was a change in her expression, a retreat that left only her features, nothing of herself. She said, "All right, you're the sheriff. What's that got to do with me? I'm twenty-one and it's legal for me to work here."

She was wise—tough, he decided. Too wise and too tough for the years she claimed. He saw an uncertainty behind the toughness and debated being equally tough. He decided against it because it was distasteful to him to assume the Cossack posture unless it was absolutely necessary and because he considered her hardness to be sham.

He asked quietly, "You a friend of Lucy Carter?" He watched her as he asked the question. The identification of the dead girl on the Kingsbridge Pike as Lucy Carter was undoubtedly in the late editions of the Clay City *Inquirer*. It would, by this time, have been included in local news broadcasts.

She rested her tray against her thigh and stood hip-shot, looking at Masters. Apparently she had neither read the papers nor listened to any news broadcasts. "Sure I know her. She used to work here."

"You said you know her. You didn't know she's dead?"

"Dead? Lucy? No, I didn't know it. What happened to her?"

She was completely unshaken and Masters reluctantly revised his opinion of her. Her tough shell was not sham. In her way this youngster was harder than Evelyn Parks.

"We'll come to that," he said. "I understand that you knew her fairly well. We want to get in touch with her people, of course. Did she ever tell you where she came from?"

She shook her head. "I don't know anything. She never said where she came from. She just drifted in here one day looking for a job and Benny took her on. A couple of weeks ago she quit."

"Why did she quit?"

They both heard the sound of footsteps on the hardtop. A stocky man in white duck pants and a white shirt with rolled up sleeves was walking swiftly, almost running, toward them. His forearms were hairy and corded with muscle. His face was hard and expressionless with small, shrewd eyes set deep beneath the temples. Hazel King said, "Here's Benny. Why don't you ask him?"

Masters had recognized Benny Zurich and he knew

at what moment Benny, in turn, recognized him. Zurich slowed his pace and affected an attitude of almost theatrical unconcern. Total innocence, Masters thought, knowing Zurich's front to be an old con trick. Benny had the gray look of the old con himself. No spirit there. No humanity, either.

Benny said, "Hello, Sheriff. Saw you drive up. What can we do for you?"

"Get off it, Benny," Masters said disgustedly.

Zurich stepped closer to Masters and folded his heavy arms across his chest. "Have it your way then," he said. "What do you want here? You haven't got a beef against this place that you can make stick." He turned to the waitress. "Hazel, you get on back inside."

Masters' temper flared but he restrained it. "She stays, Benny. This is a murder investigation."

Benny said, "You mean that Carter kid?"

Hazel King asked in a puzzled voice, "How did you know, Benny? The boy hasn't brought the papers out yet."

Zurich made a pushing motion with the palm of his hand. "Don't be dumb, kid. It's been on the radio half a dozen times." He turned again to Masters.

"You guys are all alike," Zurich complained. "Let a guy take a fall and you never forget it. What did you want to know from Hazel?"

"Not just Hazel," Masters said quietly. "I was going to get to you. What did the Carter girl give you for an address when she came to work here?"

Benny laughed, a barking facsimile of a laugh. "What do you think I'm running here—the Brown Derby? I don't ask these kids where they come from. If they want to work they get their meals and tips. I ain't got any paper on any of 'em."

Hazel King clutched at Benny's bare forearm. "What is all this?" she demanded. "What happened to Lucy?"

Benny said impatiently, "She got herself killed," and Hazel dropped her hand from his arm. Watching her, Masters saw her face grow thoughtful.

Benny continued: "Look, Masters. She had a nice shape and a pretty face. That's all I needed to know about her."

"She was here Saturday night in a car," Masters said. "You keep quiet, Benny. Who was she with, Hazel?"

The girl did not look toward Benny before she answered. She was not taking cues. "How should I know?" she answered. "She knew lots of men. If it will help you any, she called him Cliff. That much I remember. And it wasn't his car; it was a rental. They were going up to Atlanta and she was kidding him about how much mileage they were going to run up."

"Did she act as if he were an old friend?"

Benny said, "Any man in pants was a friend of Lucy's. Hazel's dumb if she don't know that."

Hazel wheeled on him. "Shut up," she said curtly. "I don't know where you get the nerve to tell me I'm dumb."

Masters waited for his answer, not speaking. Benny was aging, he thought. Letting this kid read him off was an indication. There had been a time when his reaction would have been both primitive and immediate.

Hazel continued: "I never saw her with the guy she was with before. She probably just met him."

Benny, having lost dominance over the girl, seemed also to have lost some of his own tough confidence. He said in a voice that was thready, almost whining, "I don't see what that's got to do with it, Masters. She wasn't killed Saturday night. She was killed Sunday." He added hastily, "That's what it said on the radio."

"You listened pretty carefully. How long did she work

here?" He asked the question as a test and got his answer. Hazel King spoke first.

"I already told you how long she worked here. Till about two weeks ago."

Hazel was obviously carrying the ball. Masters said, "And I already asked you something. Why did she quit? You tell me, Benny."

"She got sore. Some of the characters that come here act up with the girls. They got to take it—that's the kind of business it is. The Carter kid didn't want any more of it, so she quit. There wasn't any hard feelings."

Masters said, "You heard on the radio that she was killed Sunday night, Benny. Probably some time before midnight. I suppose you were right here at the Drive-In, surrounded by friends."

Zurich grinned. "Damn right I was here and I can produce a lot of people that saw me. You'd swear to it, wouldn't you, Hazel?"

It was not as simple as that, Masters knew. A sweeping alibi of the type volunteered by Benny Zurich could be, more often than not, pounded full of holes once a small breech was made. He would have had to be absent only a comparatively brief part of a long evening to have killed the Carter girl. Still, his alibi, such as it was, had a nuisance value for the present. He could bring Benny in and book him, but he could not conceivably hold him for more time than it would take Zurich to get a lawyer over to the courthouse. Since he had a valid line of investigation in the man Hazel had called Cliff, he decided to take no further action against Benny at the moment. He questioned Benny and Hazel for an additional few minutes and then drove away. They had not moved from the spot where he left them when he glanced into the rearview mirror a hundred yards from the Drive-In. Benny was half turned to face Hazel King. And his face was not pleasant.

There were two automobile rental agencies in Clay City. The attendant at the first of these listened closely to Masters and then nodded his head. "Sure," he said. "I remember. Cliff, you say? Wait a minute while I look it up." He turned to study the pages of a register on the counter, looking up triumphantly to say, "I knew one of our cars made a long trip Saturday night. Guy's name was Joseph Clifford. He had a credit card. Home address, 906 Albert Street, Birmingham. Representing the Fisher Roofing Company. He flew in, Sheriff. I remember he mentioned it. The car was signed out at 6:00 p.m. Saturday and in at 2:00 a.m. Sunday. Rolled up almost two hundred and fifty miles."

The Everett House, one of the city's better hotels, was located only two blocks from the rental agency. Masters, guessing that Clifford, at 2:00 a.m., would not have felt like walking any greater distance and would have kept the car had he been staying at a more distant hotel, checked at the registration desk.

The clerk was helpful. "Oh, yes. Mr. Clifford stayed with us. He arrived Saturday afternoon. Left a call for seven a.m. Sunday. We made a reservation for him on the eight o'clock plane for Birmingham."

He would have done just that if he were a casual visitor to the city, Masters thought. Come into town and, being bored with the prospect of a long evening, hunt up some quick company. That was Saturday night, though. And Doc Adams had said that she was killed Sunday night. For a moment he wondered if the coroner could have been mistaken by a great many hours. He rejected the proposition almost as soon as it entered his mind. Doc Adams was getting along; certainly he was old-fashioned, but Masters knew that he could place complete reliance on any estimate that Adams made—within minutes, not hours. On the matter of Clifford there was work to be done yet. The fact that he had made a plane reservation was not conclusive. He might have become involved in some way with Lucy Carter and stayed in Clay City. Or he could have left and returned later on Sunday. He picked up the telephone and called the airport. Joseph Clifford, he learned, had actually boarded the Birmingham plane on Sunday morning.

The second call took longer. Masters asked for a long-distance line to Birmingham and requested that the charges be transferred to his official phone. The sergeant who took the call became alert and co-operative when Masters explained that his call involved a murder investigation.

"Clifford left here by air early Sunday morning," Masters said. "The girl was killed sometime Sunday night or very early Monday morning. What I'd like you to do is locate him arriving on the plane and verify that he stayed in Birmingham until a late hour Sunday—or that he didn't."

The Birmingham sergeant promised to call back in the morning. Masters hung up, nodded his thanks to the round-eyed clerk and headed back to his office.

Lieutenant Bob Dunn was parking his laboratory trailer when Masters swung in to the curb behind him. The sheriff waited until he had completed the job and then opened the door of the Bureau car. Dunn was a small, dapper man with quick brown eyes and nicotine-stained, nervous fingers.

Masters put out his hand. "You made fair time," he said.

Dunn nodded. "Traffic was light. How have you been, Ed?"

"Fine. Up until this morning."

Dunn cocked his head. "I listened to the car radio on the way down," he said. "I understand you identified her. What was the name—Carter?"

"Lucy Carter. That's all I have got. I'm still trying to locate relatives, if any. I'd like to do that before I do anything else. You can help me out, I hope. All I know right now is that she may have come from upstate. She lived in a cheap hotel here in town."

"Did you go through her room yet?"

"Yes. I didn't find much."

"Any labels on the clothes?"

"Local. They don't mean much."

"Letters? Bills?"

Masters shook his head. "It's hard to believe, Bob, but I don't think there was a scrap of writing in the whole room. I'm about ready to believe that it was deliberate, that she made a conscious effort to conceal her background. The only thing on paper was a photograph, an old one, apparently. I couldn't get any code numbers from it."

Dunn nodded. "Probably developed and printed in a small shop somewhere where the volume is so low they don't have to use a code. Do you have any idea who did it, Ed?"

Masters felt for his pipe. "No. She was with a man on the night before she was killed. He left town the morning of her death. I'm doing what I can to either implicate or eliminate him. The girl worked for a local tough for a while. Fellow named Benny Zurich. He beat one of his waitresses up pretty bad a year or so ago but I never could prove it. I'll tell you more about him later. He's got an alibi of sorts for Sunday night. I'm going to take it apart, minute by minute." Masters had been holding his cold pipe. Now he lit it and said, "I'd like it to be Benny."

Dunn asked, "Did you take him in?"

Masters shook his head. "Not yet. Not with what I've got to make a charge on. If I picked him up now he'd holler 'persecution,' and he'd have some justification."

The two men had entered the sheriff's office, still talking. Masters introduced Dunn to Jake Bowen. When Bowen started to leave, Masters stopped him. "Wait a little while, Jake. Lieutenant Dunn and I will probably be going out again right away and I'd like you to keep store at least until Tom gets back."

Dunn had not taken a chair; instead he stood beside Masters' desk, drumming impatiently with his fingertips on its surface. Masters said, "What will it be first—the place where we found her or the place where she lived?"

"Where is she—in the morgue?"

The sheriff nodded.

"Then she can wait. I'd like to take a look at her room. After that I'll go out to the morgue with my equipment. I'll want fingernail scrapings and an autopsy report. I don't have to tell you that whatever I find will be pretty much negative evidence, Ed. It won't be much good unless you get somebody into court."

Masters smiled. "You're set on seeing that room. What is it that you think I missed?"

Dunn shrugged his slender shoulders. "You missed something, Ed. I don't believe it would be possible for anyone, let alone a girl such as she apparently was, to start a new life from scratch without retaining something of the old one. You say there was a photograph. From the way you spoke of it you think it was an old one. What was it, a family group?"

"I'd say so."

"Maybe we can get it printed up and put out as a circular all through the Southeast. Somebody would probably recognize it. But I don't think it will be necessary to go to that trouble. I'll find something in that room—or somebody will come forward when we get the regular newspaper reaction." Dunn lit a cigarette. "You puzzle me just a little, Ed. You have this fellow she was with Saturday night to look up. You have it on your mind that this Benny Zurich is a suspect. At the same time you're hitting hard to find out where she came from—as if the answer to her death lies in her past before she ever came to Clay City. How long had she lived here?"

"She came here three months ago. Three months before that she had a baby," Masters said. "She didn't have a wedding ring on and there was no mark on her finger to indicate that she ever wore one for any period of time. Since she came here she made her living as a sort of border-line prostitute. I grant you that her way of life could have set up a motive for her death in the time she was here." Masters knocked his pipe out against the desk. "But it's also possible that a situation that led to her having a baby of which there is no trace and made her cut away from her past life might have led to murder." He stood up. "I want to keep that in mind in case Benny Zurich's alibi stands up and Joseph Clifford stayed home in Birmingham Sunday night."

"Are you arresting Benny Zurich, Ed?" The voice was a new one. Masters looked up to see Charlie Hess standing in the doorway. "Can I come in or is it a private conference?" he asked.

Masters felt a mild irritation. "You're already in," he pointed out. He waved his hand toward Dunn. "Charlie, meet Lieutenant Dunn of the Bureau. Bob, this is Charlie Hess. He's a reporter with the *Inquirer*. About to be a bridegroom, Charlie is. Explains why he's such a go-getter."

Hess came all the way into the room to shake hands with Dunn. Dunn asked politely, "When's the big day?"

"In the fall sometime. I'm due for a promotion to the city desk. I'll be able to afford it then."

Masters said, "You'll get by, Charlie. Last edition out yet?"

Hess nodded.

Masters continued: "We still don't know where this girl came from, Charlie. I suppose the story went out to the wire services?"

"The first story did," Hess said. "Before we had an identification. When we did get an identification we filed an add to the wire copy but the time would be bad for the afternoon papers and I doubt if the morning papers will give it much of a play."

Masters said regretfully, "I sort of hoped we might get some help from the newspaper stories. Actually, we don't even know for certain that the name was her real one." He turned to Dunn. "Let's get on down to the hotel and look at that room. Charlie, you keep in touch. I'll let you know whatever we turn up. We're not going to arrest Zurich—not yet."

Masters brought Dunn up to date as they drove downtown and parked across from the Oceanus House. There was a new room clerk on duty. Masters spoke to him briefly. The man—an oldster this time—knew, or professed to know, less of Lucy Carter than his predecessor. "These girls, Sheriff, they come and go. I don't know anything about 'em and I don't want to know anything about 'em."

Before they went upstairs Masters asked for the number of Evelyn Parks' room. It was 308, two doors from the room that had been Lucy Carter's. The two men went upstairs and the sheriff put the key in the lock of Room 304. He turned the key and then the knob, but the door refused to open. He pushed at it again, lifting at the same time, and the door swung open.

Masters had had a terrier once. Dunn, moving swiftly about the room, picking an article up, looking at it, putting it down and moving on, reminded him of that terrier. Once Dunn plunged into the closet and emerged with an armful of dresses. "You sure these are all local labels, Ed?" he asked.

"Positive."

Dunn disappeared into the closet again. This time he came out with his hands full of shoes. Several pairs of black pumps and a battered pair of brown-and-white saddle oxfords. Masters pictured Lucy Carter as she would have looked in the oxfords. The pumps didn't fit his picture. Dunn asked hopefully, "Did you look at these?"

"I know what you're thinking, Bob. I looked. Those are cheap shoes. The numbers were stamped on in ink, not embossed into the leather. There aren't any that you can read. Do you think you can bring them out with your equipment?"

"I doubt it." Dunn frowned. "How about the ones she had on when you found her?"

Masters swore. "I missed it, Bob. You keep on looking here. I'll go down to the lobby and call the morgue." Five minutes later he had Billy on the wire at the morgue. He told him what he wanted and waited impatiently.

Billy said finally, "Sheriff Masters? I looked at those shoes. They're Tru-Mode brand. It's written in gold letters on the inner sole. There are a lot of numbers. You got a pencil ready?"

The sheriff had started for the elevator to go back to the third floor when he heard his name called. He turned to see Evelyn Parks coming toward the elevator. On the way up he said, "I was going to ask you to come to the Carter girl's room. Do you think you can remember her clothes well enough to tell if any particular dress is missing?"

She shrugged. "I've got plenty of time. I doubt if I can help you, though."

At the door to Room 304 she said, as Masters reached for the knob, "You have to lift up on it." He did so, remembering the trouble he had had with the door when he and Dunn first entered.

Inside the room he said ruefully to Dunn, "Here they are."

Dunn snatched the paper from his hand. "I'll see you at your office later on, Ed. Where is the nearest shoe store where I could get a catalogue of manufacturers?"

Masters told him and he dashed for the door and was gone.

Evelyn Parks looked at the dresses that Lieutenant Dunn had returned to the closet. She came out shaking her head. "I couldn't say, Sheriff. I recognize some of them. If you were to show me a dress and ask me if it had belonged to Lucy, the chances are that I could say yes or no. As it is—I'm sorry."

"That's all right," Masters said. "Forget about the dresses. You said an odd thing when we talked with George Cox earlier, Evelyn. You said you didn't know him 'socially.' Were you being sarcastic? I get the impression that Cox knew a lot about this place and the people in it."

She had half turned to leave the room. At Master's question she turned back to face him. "Look. You're law. He's law. What do you want me to do—cut my own throat? You're all alike."

Masters said stolidly, "Cox has nothing to do with my kind of law."

She answered bitterly. "Sure. You're sheriff and he's a city cop. You think I never ran into a sheriff before?"

He continued quietly, "There's another difference."

She kept her face averted and said nothing, and Masters knew that he could not reach her now. Later, perhaps, but not now. He said wearily, "Let it go," and walked quietly from the room.

CHAPTER FOUR

Dunn and Masters walked into the sheriff's office at five-thirty. Dunn went at once to the telephone while Masters talked in a low voice with Jake Bowen, pooling his knowledge of Benny Zurich with the deputy.

Bowen remembered the assault case of a year ago. "Fell out of a car, my butt," he grumbled. "Zurich beat her up. I've had half a dozen guys that saw it happen tell me that."

Masters said sourly, "But."

"But they won't tell it in court."

Masters said thoughtfully, "Just the same, she did work there once. Take a ride out there tonight, Jake, and see if you can get the straight of it from one of the waitresses. Zurich says she just quit. There's a waitress by the name of Hazel that knew the girl. I doubt like hell if you'll get any information from her or from Benny but give it a try. And get the names of the people Benny claims were with him Sunday night."

Bowen left the office. Dunn, after a few more minutes, hung up the telephone. "I ran up a bill for the county," he said. "Tru-Mode shoes are made in Memphis."

Masters said dryly, "County's lucky. They make a ton of shoes in Brockton, Massachusetts."

Dunn stood up. "You can have your chair back," he said. "I got the factory on the telephone just before quitting time. The shoes you found on the Carter girl were sold to a distributor in Atlanta. Where is Simontown, Ed?"

Masters frowned. "Simontown? That would be six miles northwest of here. Not much more than a crossroads town. What about it?"

"That's where the distributor sold the shoes. Dreyer's store." Dunn pushed the telephone toward Masters.

"Try it. Those country stores stay open late."

Masters, after a few moments, got through to Dreyer's store. A voice, faintly petulant, came through the buzz of a poor connection. "Yes? This is Jim Dreyer. Who is this?"

Masters identified himself. "You bought some Tru-Mode shoes—from a wholesaler in Atlanta. I don't know how long ago. Do you remember selling a pair to a girl named Lucy Carter?"

"Certainly do. I got stuck with them shoes. Too high-priced for the kind of customers I get. Gave 'em to Lucy for what they cost me, poor kid." Dreyer paused. "Now how did you happen to know Lucy bought them here?"

Masters ignored the question and asked one of his own. "Why do you call her 'poor kid'?"

The voice at the other end of the wire sputtered. "Guess you don't know Lucy or Joachim Carter either. Wouldn't ask a question like that if you did. Lucy staying down there in Clay City, is she?"

Masters said, "She's dead, Mr. Dreyer." After a moment he continued: "When did you see her last?"

Dreyer answered, "About a year ago. Just before her old man run her off."

Masters asked a few more questions and closed out the conversation with a request that Dreyer not mention the call. "It may not be the same girl," he said. "We wouldn't want to upset her parents unnecessarily. I'll be up there in the morning with a picture."

Masters put down the telephone to see Dunn watching him quizzically. Dunn said, "A call to the local sheriff would have cleared your skirts, Ed. Why do you want to go to Simontown yourself?"

"Like I told Dreyer," Masters said, "it may not be the same girl." Dunn looked skeptical, and Masters stood up and stretched before he pushed his hands deep into his pockets. "All right," he said. "It's the same girl. Any other assumption would be far-fetched. Call it a whim, my wanting to go up there. Still, she did have a baby six months ago according to the coroner—and Dreyer claims that she left home about a year ago. The baby was conceived while she was living in Simontown and it's still a fair guess that that conception and her murder are related. I'd be doing a little less than my whole job if I didn't look into it myself." He reached for his hat. "Too late for you to go to the morgue now. Let's go home and eat."

Driving toward Martha Lafferty's house, Masters thought about what he had referred to as his whim and knew that it was more than that. He had not defined it in its entirety for Dunn because it was too closely tied to a wish that he still considered partly based on sentiment. He wanted to see the house where Lucy Carter had lived when the picture on the cheap hotel dresser had been taken—wanted to see and talk to the other people in the picture. These things he wanted partly as a law-enforcement officer and partly as Ed Masters the man. As sheriff he wanted, as he had told Dunn, to find out if he could who had been responsible for Lucy Carter's pregnancy. That man, he assured himself, would be in need of an alibi.

Masters had forgotten something. He remembered it as he and Dunn got out of the car. "I'll get the hard side of Martha's tongue," he said. "Forgot to tell her I was bringing you home."

Martha Lafferty had been seventeen years old when she married Charlie Lafferty and came to live in the big house on Oak Street. That had been long enough ago so that the wooden lacework festooning the eaves of the Lafferty place had been considered high style. Twenty years of hard drinking had killed Charlie Lafferty, and Martha had turned the place into a boarding house in order to raise money to meet the taxes. Nearing seventy years now, she had lost none of the buoyancy that had endeared her to Charlie so long ago, nor any of the high spirits that had kept her young through the hard times that had followed his death. She showed some of this spirit to Masters.

"I must say that you might let a body know you were having a stranger to supper, Ed Masters. Not that I'd put myself out to make anything special but I could have had time to get the back room ready."

He grinned down at her. "Lieutenant Dunn wouldn't want anything special, Martha. Anyhow, I bet what we're having will be almost as good as he could get at the Terminal House."

Her brown eyes flashed. "The Terminal House! Any time I don't set a better table than that—that food factory—" She realized that he was teasing her and grinned back at him.

Dunn was extravagant in his praise of the food. When he had finished he pushed his chair back, sighed and shook his head. "Any time you want to open a restaurant in Atlanta, Mrs. Lafferty, you just let me know. I'll raise the money."

Later the two men sat on the wide front porch drinking beer and talking in the gathering dusk. Both men fell silent as the figure of a man appeared at the end of the walk. "Come on up, Tom," Masters called.

Tom Danning, his chief deputy, came up the walk. Masters introduced him to Dunn. When Danning had a cold beer of his own and was seated on the top step Masters asked, "Find out anything?"

Danning tasted his beer gratefully. "A little," he said. "Most of it just verifies what we already know. I talked to Hansen, told him that we could find out where he was Sunday night without too much trouble. Ed, I think he would have come in to us anyway if I hadn't gone out there. He had it on his conscience."

Masters said, "He made a run up north that night?"

Danning nodded. "Picked up three cases of liquor in town Saturday night. The way he tells it, he left his house Sunday night about sundown and got back about eleven. When he was putting his car away he saw headlights down the road, just about where we found the girl's body. There was a car stopped there. After a few minutes the car came up toward his place. It was in second gear, going hard and he says it sounded like a heavy car. The driver slammed on the brakes in front of Hansen's house and used his driveway to turn around in. Then he headed back toward town, driving fast."

Masters asked quickly, "Did he get the license number?"

Danning said, "No. He didn't have any reason to from what he knew then. He couldn't identify the make of the car either." Danning paused and then asked, "How did you make out, Ed?"

"We found out where she came from. I'm going to head up there tomorrow morning. You hold down the office until I get back, Tom."

Masters was awake and dressed before the rest of the household on the following morning. He drove toward his office, stopping only for coffee. He stopped in the office only briefly, taking the pictures of Lucy

Carter that he had arranged to have brought from the morgue. Halfway out of town he glanced at the fuel gauge. The needle was wandering toward the quarter mark. He swore impatiently and turned in at a neighborhood filling station. When the attendant came out, wiping his hands on a piece of waste, Masters said, "Morning, Tommy. Fill it up, will you?"

He got out, while Tommy pumped the gasoline, and kicked desultorily at the tires. Now that he was committed to the trip to Simontown he more than half regretted his decision to go. There were a lot of things to be done. The Birmingham police would be calling about Joe Clifford. Jake Bowen might have picked up something at Benny's Drive-In. He stepped back against his own car as another car drove in to stop beside the pump island. He heard Tommy say, "Hello, Charlie," and glanced up to see Charlie Hess getting out of the other car.

"Put in five, Tommy," Hess said.

Tommy, with professional gravity, said, "All right, Charlie. But you ought to get that tank fixed. It's dangerous to ride around like that." Charlie, at that moment, recognized Masters. He walked toward the sheriff. "Got a leak in my gas tank where the filler pipe pulled loose," he said. "If I put more than five gallons in at a time it sloshes around and leaks out. Where you headed, Ed?"

"North a ways," Masters said.

"Anything new on the Carter business?"

"Nothing you haven't got, Charlie."

Hess braced one foot on the bumper of Master's car. "You were talking about Benny Zurich with Lieutenant Dunn yesterday, Ed. You could do a lot worse than work on the angle that he might have done it. She used to work for him, you know."

Masters said, "I know." He waited for Charlie Hess

to continue, volunteering nothing himself.

Hess said, "You know what kind of a place Zurich runs, Ed. It's common knowledge. We've been kicking around the thought of doing a piece on it. You know the kind. 'Our fair city's shame,' sort of thing. That Benny is a tough man, Ed. We looked up his record. It's as long as your arm. He must have paid through the nose to get a license."

Masters, watching Hess, frowned. "I don't follow you, Charlie," he said. "Benny is a bad article. That place he runs smells from here to Florida, but I can't get a murder indictment on the strength of that."

Hess straightened. "That's not what I meant, Ed. I don't mean to try and tell you how to run your office. What I mean is, if you backtrack to the time she worked there and if you extend your formal investigation to include Benny's place, we can use that as a peg to hang a story on. Maybe get his license. The county commissioners wouldn't openly back him in the face of that kind of publicity."

Masters shook his head. "I couldn't do that, Charlie. We've already been looking into a possible connection between the Carter girl and Benny's place, but if you went ahead and said I was investigating you'd be violating the rules of my office—and my personal confidence. I think your paper's attorney would also tell you that you'd be risking a libel suit. Benny is smart as well as tough."

The attendant said, "All set, Sheriff. Put it on the county account?"

Masters got into his car. "Do that," he said. He nodded to Hess and put the car into gear.

He thought briefly about Charlie as he headed out of town, increasing speed as he passed through the outskirts. Charlie was eager—"pushy," Martha Lafferty would have called him. Couldn't really hold that against him, Masters mused, especially since he was getting married in the fall and wanted a better job. He wondered momentarily if Charlie had just happened to stop in for gas or if he had seen the county car and decided to try to pump the sheriff about his destination. Well, even so, he thought, the man was just doing his job.

His wristwatch showed nine-thirty when Masters eased his pressure on the accelerator and slowed the car at the outskirts of Simontown. It was a hamlet, rather than a town, and just now it was drowsing in the early morning heat. A scattering of small houses, some of them unpainted, were the first indication of the existence of the town. Shortly the road divided, splitting itself against a common ornamented with a bandstand and a handful of dusty chinaberry trees. Massed against the right fork were half a dozen stores, a movie theater and a bank. Along the left-hand road were more ornate houses and, where the roads converged again, a white-columned building that Ed recognized as the courthouse. He drew up before it, picked up his pictures of Lucy Carter and got out of the car.

Sheriff Byrd wore a long and drooping mustache under sharp blue eyes, undimmed by his sixty years. Masters, remembering him from a half-dozen peace-officers' conventions, knew that the mustache was a condescension to back-country politics, a trade mark. He also knew Sam Byrd as a capable and efficient sheriff. He took the proffered chair and disposed of the customary greetings.

Byrd said finally, "Now I know damn well you didn't come clear up here to Davis County just to say hello, Ed. I also know you wish I'd stop fence mending so you could get to the point. All right then—what's on your mind?"

"Business, Sam. A girl was murdered down in Clay City Sunday. It looks as if she might have come from Simontown."

Byrd raised bushy eyebrows. "That so? Read about the killing in the Atlanta paper. Just a small item from the Associated Press. Don't believe the body was identified, time the piece was written."

"It probably wasn't," Masters said. "We didn't get an identification ourselves until afternoon. The girl's name was Lucy Carter. Do you know her?" He slid the glossy photographs across the desk.

Byrd picked them up. His mouth tightened as he studied them and his ancient blue eyes narrowed. "That's Lucy Carter," he said at length. "Hair is different and she's plucked her eyebrows. Looks older somehow. But that's her. Who did this to her, Ed?"

Masters shook his head. "I don't know, Sam. Thought maybe you could help me if it was someone from around here that had reason to hate her. That's why I came up myself. Figured I'd talk to you and find out for sure if it was her; then we'd both go tell her family."

Byrd nodded. "Fair enough. Nobody around here had any reason to hate Lucy, though. Never had any boyfriends. Girlfriends either. Her pa is back-county hard and he kept her pretty much to home. She ran off a year or so ago."

Masters said, "I know," and, when Sam Byrd glanced at him in surprise, explained about his call to Jim Dreyer.

When he finished Byrd chuckled. "'Say this much," he said. "You ain't been asleep." He stood up and reached in the desk drawer for a pistol in a worn leather a holster. He strapped it about his lean waist and grinned. "Voters around here have got used to seeing me dress like Wyatt Earp," he said. "Can't afford to disappoint 'em in an election year. Yep—Lucy ran away from home. Joachim—that's her pa—came in and told us about it. Told us he didn't want her back, as a matter of fact. Some say he drove her off."

Masters knocked his pipe out against his heel. "That so?"

"Yep. I figure you'll understand better when you meet Joachim."

They walked out to Masters' car and drove off, Byrd giving directions. Three miles outside of town Masters, following instructions, turned off onto a red clay road that branched from the state highway. Another mile and they came to a weather-beaten frame house set in the middle of a ten-acre plot planted in bell peppers and peanuts. The front porch sagged drearily and the glass was gone from an upstairs window, so that the ramshackle building seemed to leer at them. Masters pulled the car up. While they got out he studied the grounds and the outbuildings. There was a barn, sagging along a broken-backed roof beam, and a shed with three sides. A decrepit Buick touring car was parked inside the shed. There was an atmosphere of neglect and poverty to the farm that was repellent. Byrd broke the silence.

"Ain't any need for the place to look like this, come right down to it. Old Joachim's got more money than any three men in Simontown."

As he spoke a young man came out to meet them from behind the barn. About twenty, he was dressed only in overalls and a pair of heavy, clumsy shoes. His uncut hair was long and his face was sullen.

"You want Pa? He's up in the back lot," he said. His face remained completely expressionless.

Byrd nodded. "This is Abel Carter—Lucy's brother," he said to Masters. He continued, talking this time to the youth: "Be obliged if you'd ask your pa to step down here, Abel."

The youth's eyes had flickered briefly at the mention of Lucy but he merely turned away, saying nothing, and strode away toward the back of the house. The two men continued up to the porch and knocked on the warped, paint-peeling door. A woman opened it. Assuming that she was Lucy Carter's mother, she ought to be in her early forties, Ed Masters thought, but work and futility had intensified the lines and stresses of age so that she looked much older. Her eyes held the sheriff. They were opaque and as lifeless as the eyes of a corpse. They held nothing. No hope. Not even hopelessness. Both men raised their hats.

"Howdy, Miz Carter," Byrd said. "This is Sheriff Masters from Clay County."

She nodded, not speaking, and with no interest reflected in her sallow face. Byrd continued: "Sheriff Masters is here on official business, so to speak. We asked Abel to ask Joachim to step down here."

Something stirred in the lifeless eyes. Watching intently, Masters could not have said what emotion it was or if it was an emotion. She smoothed her apron nervously with her hands. "Come in then," she said. She led the way into a front room that was musty-smelling from disuse.

The two men took seats and waited uncomfortably, feeling that polite small talk would be wasted on this gaunt woman. Masters surveyed the room, taking in the horsehair set and the marble-topped table with the great Bible placed precisely in its middle. He had seen a thousand such rooms among the country people of Clay County but he could recall none of them as having had quite the oppressive atmosphere of the Carter parlor. He was relieved—and he suspected that Sam Byrd felt the same sensation—when heavy footsteps echoed from the porch and Joachim Carter strode into the room followed by his son.

He was taller than Masters. Like his son he was dressed in overalls, but beneath his he wore a heavy suit of underwear, stained with perspiration and gray with dust. His face too was gray, almost as gray as his sparse hair. Deep lines trisected it from his nose to his jaws and his mouth was clamped tightly above a weak chin. When he spoke Masters had a glimpse of blackened stubs of teeth.

"What call do you have taking a man from his toil?" he demanded.

Byrd shifted in his chair. "This is Sheriff Masters from Clay County," he said. "He'll tell you why we're here."

Carter turned impatiently toward Masters, who said uncomfortably, "It's about your daughter." Carter interrupted him. "I have no daughter," the gaunt man said.

Byrd stood up. "Now look here, Joachim," he said chidingly, "I know how you feel about Lucy. Still and all, she was your own flesh and blood."

From her chair in the corner of the room Mrs. Carter called out, "What you mean, 'was'?"

Joachim turned on her savagely. "Shut your mouth, woman!" he cried and turned back to face Masters and Byrd. "I have no daughter," he repeated.

Abel Carter had been standing in the doorway, unmoving. Now he stepped into the room. In a low voice he said, "Hear them out, Pa."

Masters, moving quietly, placed the photograph of Lucy Carter on the marble-topped table. "This girl was found dead yesterday morning," he said. "Sheriff Byrd thinks it's your daughter."

Abel Carter was the first to move. He picked up the print and studied it briefly, then, without speaking, he turned and bolted from the room. Mrs. Carter watched him go. "She was the only thing he cared about," she said wearily. She moved toward the table and looked at the picture almost casually. Then she nodded. "That's her," she said. "What happened to my girl?"

Masters shook his head mutely and she turned to Joachim. She kept her voice flat, toneless. "It's Lucy, Joachim. Prettier'n she ever was when you had her choppin' cotton and weedin' corn. Skin's almost white."

Carter had remained motionless while his wife and son looked at the picture. Now he repeated stubbornly—a shade uncertainly this time, Masters thought—"I have no daughter."

She carried the picture to him and thrust it in front of his eyes. "Look at her, Joachim. Go ahead and look at her and say it isn't your daughter."

He glanced quickly at the picture and turned away "I had a daughter once," he said. "Don't torment me, woman."

Mrs. Carter laughed bitterly. Masters, studying her, knew that she was only a step from hysteria, that only some stronger emotion than grief kept her from breaking.

"Torment you, Joachim? Didn't you torment her for twenty years? Didn't you take her out of high school to make her work on the farm? Didn't you make her dress like a slut from the Corners?" She sighed wearily. "Twenty years and she never had a pretty new dress for herself. Never had boys callin' to court her, and her prettier'n any girl in Simontown. Time she did torment you, Joachim."

Carter cried out, "Give me peace, woman! I only did what a just man would do. The Good Book says if your right hand offendeth thee, cut it off. If thy right eye offendeth thee, pluck it out!"

She continued in the same monotone: "Why don't you pray, Joachim? Pray like you did the night you turned her out after you beat her with a harness strap until she fainted?"

While Masters and Byrd watched in revulsion, Carter did just that. Suddenly he dropped to his knees and began a maudlin prayer as tears streamed down his weathered cheeks.

"Oh, Lord," he cried. "Turn this woman from her sinful ways. Teach her respect for the master of this house...."

The nasal voice droned on while Mrs. Carter beckoned to the officers. They followed her out to the kitchen.

"He'll go on like that for an hour," she said dully. "Then he'll lay hands on me. Now tell me what happened to my daughter."

Masters saw the first glimmer of expression in her eyes. It was not grief. Briefly he stated the facts concerning Lucy's death, omitting that she had had a baby. There would be time for that later—if it became necessary—and in the meantime, this woman had enough to contend with.

"You accused your husband of turning her out," he said finally. "He told Sheriff Byrd that she ran away."

She shrugged. "There was a fella Lucy met while he was fishing in the Oconee," she said. "Lots of people come for the fishing. Weren't nothin' to it, much. Lucy didn't know many boys. He"—she gestured toward the front room where they could still hear Carter's voice rising and falling—"wouldn't let 'em come to call. One day he caught 'em down on the river bank. Lucy and this fella. Wasn't doin' nothing but holding hands the way young folks do. He dragged her home and accused her of laying with the boy. She flew right back at him and said as how she was going to marry him. That's when he up and hit her with the strap. Wasn't the first time but this time he acted like he was crazy: her layin' there and him 'a cuttin' at her, all the time shoutin' prayers and yelling about whoremasters and sinners and fornicators. Abel finally drug him off. By and by she got up and said she wouldn't stay in this house. He told her good riddance and to get off his land."

"Did you ever hear from her after that, Mrs. Carter? It seems as if she would have written," Masters said.

She shook her head. "Maybe she did. I expect she did. Wouldn't have done any good. Joachim went out to the highway to the mailbox every day. Wouldn't let Abel or me go. If she wrote he never told us about it."

Byrd caught Masters' eye and the two officers stood up. Mrs. Carter looked down at her folded hands "When is she going to be buried?" she asked.

Masters said, "Wednesday. Eleven o'clock."

"We'll be there. Me and Abel, we'll be there."

Masters gave her the address of Gregory's undertaking parlors and the two men left the house. Before they reached the car they heard a shout. Turning, they saw Joachim Carter striding toward them.

When he came up to them his face was stern again. "Want you to know," he said, "that I'm a just man. Aim to pay my just debts. How much is it going to cost to bury that woman?"

Byrd spat on the ground and Masters felt an unholy desire to strike the man. "I don't know," he said. "The county will pay for it."

Carter shook his head stubbornly. "Aim to pay my debts," he said. "You tell them to send the bill to me." He turned and walked back toward the house while Byrd swore luridly.

"Told you he was a hard man," he said.

Masters dropped Byrd at his office after they had visited Dreyer's store. Dreyer, a rabbity little man could tell them only that he had sold the Tru-Mode shoes to Lucy Carter about a year previously. "Poor little girl never had much," he said. "She saved up for a long time for those shoes. I let her have them for what they cost me." He turned to his cash register and took out a five-dollar bill, which he handed to Masters. "You buy her some flowers," he said. "That son of a bitch of a father of hers won't send none."

As they left the store Sam Byrd shook his head. "First time I ever heard Jim Dreyer cuss."

When the two peace officers were again seated in Byrd's office, Masters asked, "Sam, do you think you could find out where Carter was on Sunday night?"

Byrd's mouth opened in surprise. Then his eyes narrowed and he stroked his jaw with his fingers. He said at length, "No, Ed. Not Joachim. He's a hard man; never saw a harder. But his own daughter? I can't see him as a killer."

Masters said dryly, "Yet, from what we heard today, he nearly beat her to death the night she left home."

Byrd shook his head. "I can try," he said. "Back-country families like the Carters don't go out Sunday nights unless it's to a revival or some such like. If I asked him he'd say he was home. He'd have his wife and the boy to back him up—they'd never dare go against his say—and that would be it."

Masters nodded. "We've got some like him down in Clay County. That's why I didn't say anything out at his place. Mrs. Carter and the boy will be down for the funeral tomorrow. It seemed to me that if I talked to them when he wasn't nearby I'd have a better chance at getting a straight answer." He stood up. "There's another thing, Sam. I didn't bring it up out there, the way things were. Lucy had a baby six months ago. Autopsy showed it. Do you know what boys she ran with?"

Sam Byrd shook his head. "Local boys were afraid of Joachim," he said. "If they saw her it was on the sly. I'll dig into it if you want."

Masters stood up and extended his hand. "I'd appreciate it," he said.

CHAPTER FIVE

Ed Masters pushed the county car hard on the return trip to Clay City. He was impatient to be back at his desk, impatient to know if the Birmingham police had called back a report on Joseph Clifford, impatient to find out if Jake Bowen had learned anything in his visit to Benny's Drive-In. A nagging uncertainty made him bite down hard on his pipestem as he wove the car in and out of the noonday traffic. It might have been smart police work to shock Joachim Carter out of his religious hysteria by a formal questioning; certainly the farmer could not be eliminated from the list of those who might have wished Lucy Carter dead. He shook his head. He had had more than one experience with Carter's type and you couldn't use textbook methods in dealing with them. He decided that he had made the right decision in holding off on Carter, and having so decided he put it from his mind.

It was one-thirty when he parked in front of the Clay County courthouse. Anxious to get to his office, he was irritated when he was hailed before he could climb the marble steps of the building. Charlie Hess hurried toward him, followed by a tall girl in a light summer dress and a wide-brimmed hat. Recognizing her as Charlie's fiancée, Masters touched the brim of his hat and smiled. He liked Sally Martin. She was on the near side of being pretty, but she had a nice carriage and a nicer manner. Worked in the bank and you'd never know from the way she acted that her father owned it. She came up behind Charlie with a smile that was half tolerant, half apologetic.

"Hello, Ed," she said. She turned to Charlie. "You hurry up now. I've had almost an hour and a half for lunch already."

Hess said impatiently, "All right, Sally. Ed, you're back sooner than we expected. What did you find out?"

Masters, making what allowance he could for Hess's zeal in his job, nevertheless wished that the reporter could be underfoot a little less often. A fair man, he supposed Charlie had a right to make the best of what was a big story for the Clay City *Inquirer* and checked the abrupt answer he felt like giving.

"I talked to her father and mother," he said. "She lived in Simontown. Ran away from home a year or so ago. Tell you what, Charlie, I've got a lot of work to do. Why don't you let me call you later?"

Hess turned away reluctantly. "All right, Ed," he said. "I'll use the home-town bit and the runaway business."

Jake Bowen and Bob Dunn were waiting for Masters in the office. Masters asked immediately, "Did you get a call from Birmingham?"

Bowen picked up a sheet of paper. "From a Sergeant Lewis," he said. "Joseph Clifford arrived home by air Sunday morning. He played golf at a country club and had dinner there with his wife. He didn't leave until almost 2:00 a.m. and when he did leave it was with his wife. Sergeant Lewis says they've been discreet in their check-up so far, Clifford being married and supposedly a solid citizen. He also says if you want them to they'll pick him up for questioning, solid citizen or not."

Masters felt an inclination to call the Birmingham department. Solid citizens like Clifford should act like

solid citizens away from home and not be getting
themselves involved with the Lucy Carters they
chanced—or arranged—to meet. Wryly he recognized
that his reaction was largely founded in his
disappointment at the failure of a promising lead. He
could make Joseph Clifford sweat for a few hours but
he would accomplish nothing by doing it. "So much
for Clifford," he said. "What about Benny's place?"

Jake grimaced. "You're going to have to square me
with my wife," he said. "She doesn't more than half
believe you sent me out there last night. The Carter
girl did work out there up to a couple of weeks ago
just the way Benny Zurich tells it. There are a few
things he left out, though." Jake held up a closed right
fist. With his left hand he unpeeled the forefinger of
the closed hand. "One: He made a big pitch for her
right after she came to work there. She didn't like
him—or his pitch—and she let him know about it,
but not until she had made a little hay out of the
situation. Among other things, he bought her a
wristwatch."

Bob Dunn smiled. "Not to interrupt," he said, "I don't
suppose Benny told you these things?"

Bowen shook his head. "Hell, no. I spent eleven bucks
and two hours with one of Benny's waitresses who
didn't know I was a deputy." He unpeeled the middle
finger. "Two: There's a girl out there by the name of
Hazel King. She came to work for Benny a little while
before the Carter girl did. She wanted Benny—don't
ask me why except that she's a wise kid and Benny's
got a good thing out there. She had a fight with the
Carter girl. Not a hair-pulling contest, but a fight just
the same. She put it up to Benny that it was her or
the Carter girl and it was then that the Carter girl
told Benny where he stood with her. This King girl
made Benny get his watch back."

Masters, when Jake Bowen paused, asked, "Did Lucy use the cabins?"

Bowen shook his head. "I don't know, Ed."

Masters, seeing Dunn's frown, explained, "Benny has a half-dozen cabins out back, Bob. He works it in a way that keeps him clear. Say a man comes in and buys a few drinks and gets friendly with one of the carhops. If the man later rents a cabin and asks that the carhop bring him his next order there, it's not up to Benny to determine if there's any misconduct. So Benny claims." Masters turned to Bowen. "This King girl. Does she handle cabin trade?"

This time Bowen made a flat answer. "No. I think she did at one time, if I can believe my waitress. Now she's Benny's property—or he's hers." He shook his head. "That King girl is tough, Ed. After I finished playing rube I went in to see Benny. I wanted the names of the people that could verify that he was there Sunday night. She horned right in, answering for Benny, taking over."

Masters nodded. "I've seen it before. There's a type of man—I'd say Benny was typical—who likes to let himself be dominated by a woman, especially if she's young and pretty. I don't mean your Milquetoast, who tolerates it; I mean your Benny type. A man who has been hard and tough all his life. One day he realizes he is getting old and being tough becomes a strain, so he accepts domination and pretends to himself that it's some prettier emotion. Bob, you've probably seen something like it in the state prison."

"I have. Mixed up with homosexuality most of the time, but I know what you mean. I've seen it in old convicts in and out of prison."

Masters turned again to Jake Bowen. "What about that alibi?"

Bowen shook his head. "One of those things. He gave

me the names of half a dozen people who were at his place. I haven't checked them yet. I'll work on it this afternoon if you say so."

"Know any of the people?"

"A few. None I'd give a character reference to."

Masters had been thoughtfully sucking at his pipe. "Let it go," he said. "There's a quicker way. Thinking about old cons reminded me of a case they had in Reidsville a year or so ago. Somebody knifed a guard in the dark during a movie showing. Turned out it was a young punk but not until after this old-timer had confessed to it. The young punk was his boy. Twist it around a little and what do you think Benny's reaction would be if we picked up Hazel King for questioning?"

Jake Bowen said slowly, "He'd go right out of his mind. If he knows anything at all he'll tell it. You'd be on shaky ground though, Ed. You couldn't hold her long."

"It wouldn't take long. I have a valid reason for bringing her in. She did know Lucy Carter and she did see her Saturday night."

"You want me to go with you?" Bowen asked.

Masters shook his head. "I'll go by myself. I'm going to try to make it about three o'clock. If I'm lucky, Benny won't be there. If he gets back there after I've picked her up and finds her gone he'll be more apt to panic. I'd take bets that he'll be here within ten minutes after he finds out." He turned to Bob Dunn. "You go out to the morgue?"

"This morning," Dunn answered. "Nothing under her fingernails. She wasn't able to reach whoever it was to rake him. Tom Danning ran me out to the place where you found her. I got some samples of soil and humus. Negative value, Ed. You catch the murderer and I'll examine his clothes. If he picked up some of that dirt and it didn't come off between then and now you might get a conviction—but only if he confesses. You can find soil and humus like that all through this part of Georgia."

"Where is Tom now?"

Bowen answered. "He's downtown, trying to find out where she was Sunday and who saw her last. Said he'd call you if he turned anything up."

Masters leaned to pull out the bottom drawer of his desk. From it he took a bottle filled with a clear liquid. He uncorked it and the pungent odor of corn whisky eddied in the room. He passed it to Dunn and Bowen in turn and then held it to his own lips.

"I don't make a habit of drinking in duty hours," he explained, "but there comes a time when a drink of shine seems like the only thing that will take a bad taste out of your mouth."

Dunn's eyes were watering. "And put a worse one in. Do you fellows drink this stuff regularly?"

Bowen pretended surprise. "Stuff, you call it? This is pretty high-grade corn. Ed and me took it from a couple of fellows up in the pine thickets. It's evidence, isn't it, Ed?"

"It is," Masters agreed. "Was, anyway."

Dunn had been studying Masters, understanding the byplay about the whisky for what it was: a deliberate effort to relax tension. "What did you find out in Simontown, Ed?" he asked.

"Actually nothing," Masters said quietly. "About the bad taste I told you about: Carter—Lucy's father—said at first he didn't have a daughter." Masters talked on for a few minutes, filling in the details of his trip.

When the sheriff had finished, Bowen asked, "Did you tell them the girl had had a baby after she ran away?"

Masters shook his head. "The Carter woman will be

here tomorrow. If it's necessary I'll tell her then." He stood up. "I've seen some men I'd like to see hang since I've been sheriff. Benny Zurich would be one. Joachim Carter is another. If we can't tie Benny to the Carter murder, I'm going to start looking in his direction."

Bowen said, "Hell, Ed. His own daughter?"

"He denied he had such a thing."

Hazel King was on duty at the Drive-In when Masters drove up. She walked to the car, tray in hand, and stood sullenly waiting for him to speak. Masters said, "I'd like you to come downtown to the courthouse with me." He dropped his glance to her brief shorts. "You might want to change into something more appropriate."

She shrugged her shoulders. "If it's about Lucy Carter, I already told you all I know. I don't see why have to go with you."

There was no fright in her voice but there was shading of uncertainty. Where Benny, veteran of dozen arrests, would have protested, this girl retained the average citizen's slight awe of an official request delivered at first hand. Masters was aware that he was in a sense, bullying the girl and he did not for an in instant regret it. She had not turned to look back toward the Drive-In proper, which signified in all probability that Benny was not there. Giving her no chance to recover her balance, he said, glancing at his watch, "You've got five minutes if you want to change."

"I've got to tell one of the other girls where I'm going," she protested. "I can't do that and change my clothes in five minutes."

Masters said, "Try."

On the trip to the courthouse she sat away from him, squeezing against the door on her side, not in an attitude of fear but rather of a form of distasteful contempt. It had taken her five more than the five minutes the sheriff had allotted her to change. She did not speak and Masters kept the silence.

He was tempted to let her sit in his office and make a pretense of questioning her while he waited for Benny but he decided against it. He had already come to the conclusion that this girl would never comprehend pity. Instead he took her down the narrow stairs that led to the cubicle of tiny cells, empty at this time by pre-arrangement. The cells were open on two sides, drab cages made of inch-thick iron rods covered with scabby aluminum paint. He doubted that she had ever seen a cell before, and for the first time she came near panic.

"You're not going to put me in there!" she cried. "God damn you, you said you just wanted to ask me some questions!"

"I do," he said quietly. "When I get around to it. How do you want to do it? I can leave you in there to wait until I'm ready to talk to you. The door will be open and you won't be charged. The other way you'll be held as a material witness and the door will be locked."

She half turned toward the stairway, poised as if to run. Then she changed her mind. She said bitterly, "I'll wait," and strode defiantly toward the nearest of the cells.

Masters said, "The jailer will be down in a few minutes. He'll get you some coffee if you want it."

She didn't answer and he went back up the stairs.

Dunn and Tom Danning were in the office. Masters grinned at them as he entered. When Dunn raised a questioning eyebrow the sheriff said, "So far, so good. I didn't have to make a charge. She's willing to answer some questions voluntarily." He glanced at his watch. "Quarter of four. Depending on the time Benny Zurich gets back to the Drive-In, we should see him in a half hour or so. Bob, I'll bet you our dinners that he'll have a lawyer with him."

Dunn shook his head and said quizzically, "You know your man. What does he need a lawyer for if you haven't made a charge against the girl?"

Masters reached for his pipe. "He doesn't know that," he said and turned to Tom Danning. "What did you find out, Tom?"

"Where she was Sunday afternoon," the deputy said "She was at the Capitol Theater. I don't know when she got up that morning, but she had breakfast in a Liggett's drugstore across the street from the Oceanus House. The clerk remembers her. She had coffee there about every morning. She went to the movie a little after one. The ticket-seller remembers her because that was another of her habits. She went to the movie every Sunday. Even remembers that she had a yellow dress on—one of those bright yellow colors that almost seems to glow, she said."

Dunn said, "One of those rhodamine dyes, probably."

Masters had forgotten to draw on his pipe. "What about after she left the movie?" he asked sharply.

Tom Danning shook his head. "Not a trace. I figured she might have gone back to her room at the Oceanus House, so I checked with the clerk. He couldn't say, one way or the other."

Dunn, who was seated in a position that allowed him to see into the hallway, said, "I think this is your friend now, Ed."

Benny Zurich came into the room, half running, trailed by a man in a brown suit. The latter had a pale, doughy face and he seemed to be trying to convey the impression that he was not actually with Zurich.

Benny shouted as he crossed the threshold, "Where is she, Masters? God damn it, this is going to cost you!"

Masters calmly greeted the man in the brown suit, "Afternoon, Counselor Parker," using the man's title for Dunn's benefit, before he turned toward the frenzied Zurich. "Where is who, Benny?"

"You know damn well who. Hazel King. You waited until I wasn't there before you picked her up. All right. I'm going to sue you for false arrest. Now get her out here! Parker says she's got a right to counsel."

Parker said diffidently, "Come now. I'm sure we can straighten this thing out without recriminations." Masters, hoping that Benny's shouting could not be heard in the cell block, said, "Hazel King was one of the last persons known to have seen Lucy Carter. She is known to have quarreled with the dead girl—"

Benny interrupted frantically. "That fight was a long time ago," he shouted. "Since you know about it, you must know that. You're just using that as a reason for framing Hazel!"

Masters continued: "Lucy Carter and Hazel King worked at the same place up until two weeks ago, saw each other almost every day."

He spoke slowly, drawing the words out, giving Benny every chance to break in, to let his temper betray him. "Then Lucy quit, for reasons that are pretty vague."

Again Benny interrupted: "Jesus Christ, Masters, those girls come and go. There's been three or four of them drifted in and worked for a few days since Lucy quit—and that's only two lousy weeks."

Counselor Parker droned, "He's quite right, Sheriff. Those people are transients in a sense. Surely we can't ask Mr. Zurich to answer for their comings and goings. As he said, there have been several of them in the comparatively short time since the Carter girl left."

"With this difference," Masters said. "As far as I

know, no one has reported finding their bodies."

Benny lowered his head and shook it like an angry bull. "That's a lot of crap, Masters. All this talk is crap." He wheeled on Parker. "And you're supposed to be a lawyer and you stand here and listen to it." He turned back to Masters. "It's easy for you to pick on ex-cons and young girls, but you don't lean on a guy like George Cox, do you? He might fight back—or else he's splitting with you."

Parker put his hand on Benny's shoulder, trying frantically to stop him from speaking further, but Zurich flung him off. Masters sought, just as hard, for a means of baiting Benny further and decided to let the man's own angry momentum carry him on.

Benny made a peculiar gesture, clutching his left biceps with his right hand. "This for us," he shouted "But you don't bother your own kind."

Bob Dunn and Tom Danning were alert to the situation. Both men faded unobtrusively from Benny's sight lest he suddenly recall what they were and where he was. Masters had a sudden, vivid recollection of the scene on yesterday afternoon when he had gone to Lucy Carter's room with George Cox. The big detective had swung the door open without difficulty; he had probably known then that the door stuck and had to be opened in a particular manner. He had probably known Lucy Carter. Nothing strange in that. The strangeness lay in his failure to indicate it.

Parker tried once again, vainly, to quiet Benny Zurich. Zurich flung him off a second time. "You let a bastard like Cox bleed me and knock down on every whore in Clay City and you don't do a damn thing about it, but you'd frame a kid like Hazel King. You want to know who killed the Carter girl, why don't you ask Cox? She had something on him that would have ruined him in this town."

Masters shook his head. "You're lying, Zurich," he said, trying to goad the man even further.

Zurich started an angry reply, caught himself and paused while he glanced around the room, noting Dunn and Tom Danning patiently waiting near the door. Masters cursed himself for the three words he had said. Apparently they had been the check Zurich needed to regain some degree of self-control.

"Let me get this straight," he said. "You were paying money to George Cox. For what?"

Parker, the attorney, said nervously, "You'd better not answer that question, Mr. Zurich." He turned to face Masters. "Don't misunderstand, Sheriff. We don't want to be uncooperative. At the same time, I have a duty to my client."

Masters looked at him coldly. "Zurich is under suspicion of murder along with Hazel King," he said. "I don't have enough evidence to hold him just now. I'll give you that. At the same time, if Zurich didn't do it, the surest way for him to prove it is to help us find out who did." He turned to face Zurich, who had lost his fire and wore once again the gray, cindery look that Masters recognized as meaning total resistance to further questioning. Because he had to try, he asked, "Can you back up your remarks about knockdowns? It can't hurt you, Benny. Not the respectable way you run that place of yours."

Zurich rich said morosely, "He took money from all the tarts on Water Street. He shook down some of my girls. I'm not going to protect the lousy thief."

"What did the Carter girl have on him?"

"I don't know. All I know is she said once that he'd better not try to go up against her because she knew somebody or something—I don't remember which it was. I put it down as smart talk and didn't pay any more attention to it."

"When did she say this?"

"I don't know," Benny said, a little desperately. "A week or so before she quit. What about Hazel, Sheriff? I helped you out." A faint whining note crept into his voice.

Masters said contemptuously, "You came in here with your lawyer making big talk about suits for false arrest. Any help you gave me you gave me because you lost your head." He signaled to Tom Danning, who disappeared into the hallway.

Parker said fussily, "The fact remains, Sheriff, that he did give your office some information that may well be of use to you. In view of that fact, I think it only fair that you cooperate in the matter of his employee Hazel King. If you have already charged her"—the attorney sucked in a breath—"I can ask Justice Fennell for a writ of habeas—"

Masters interrupted him. "Don't bother," he said wearily. "I haven't made any charges against the girl. She agreed to answer some questions for me. She can go right after that."

Hazel King walked into the room, followed by Tom Danning. Benny Zurich moved toward her, checked himself and asked warily, "You all right, Hazel?"

"I guess so," she said. Seeing Parker, she asked in bitter voice, "Can he really get away with arresting me?"

Masters grinned at her. "What did I say, Hazel? That I'd like you to come down to the courthouse with me." He turned toward Parker. "I don't believe that constitutes an arrest, counselor."

Hazel King blazed at him, "You put me in that cell."

Masters shook his head. "Not exactly. I told you if you wanted to wait, the door wouldn't be locked and you wouldn't be charged. How about it, counselor?"

Parker looked at him with some respect and then

glanced back at Benny and Hazel King. "I think you folks had better try to help the sheriff," he said.

CHAPTER SIX

A solid hour of questioning produced nothing further for Ed Masters. Benny withdrew, after Hazel King's appearance, into a shell of stubborn silence. The King girl adopted an air of insolent resentment that had Parker mopping his forehead. Adding it up, after he had regretfully dismissed the pair, Masters arrived at an equation that contained too many x's.

"There's a chance," he told Dunn, "that he's telling the truth. Cox has a bad reputation. Bad man; bad enemy; bad cop. I'll say this for him—he's fearless, physically. Whatever the Carter girl had on him—presuming that Benny Zurich was telling the truth—was something that affected him some other way. Benny as much as stated that. Remember the words he used: 'ruin him in this town'?"

Dunn shook his head. "I don't know your man Cox," he said doubtfully, "but I know a hundred like Benny. It looks to me as if he was throwing tar at Cox to keep it from getting on him."

Masters stood up. "I think I can find out," he said.

Danning warned him, "You'd better not waste any time doing it. Benny has cooled off by now. Pretty soon he's going to start worrying about the things he said about Cox, particularly since Cox seems to have something on him. He'll probably call him and warn him to cover up—if he has anything to cover up."

Masters started for the door, paused, and said to Danning, "When Jake comes back or calls in, tell him I'm pretty anxious for him to finish clearing Benny's alibi. Give him a hand if he needs it. Bob," he added,

"I'll call back. You'd better figure on eating without me."

He got into the county car and drove downtown, parking across the street from the Oceanus House. The young desk clerk with the bloodshot eyes was on duty again. Masters stopped at the desk briefly. "Is the Parks woman in?" he asked.

The clerk shrugged. "How should I know?" he asked peevishly.

Ed Masters was tired and irritated by his frustrating interview with Benny Zurich. The clerk's insolence tore the fragile thread of his temper. "Well, damn," he said softly. "What's your name?"

The clerk, warned by the change in Masters' inflection, became belatedly polite. "Shaw, Sheriff," he said, "Ernest Shaw. I think the Parks girl is in. Wait a minute and I'll go and see."

Masters shook his head. "Let it go," he said. "Shaw, I'll give you a piece of advice. Don't slow me up next time. Don't be smart. Just give me whatever information I ask you for. You remember that, will you?"

Shaw nodded his head mutely.

Masters continued: "I may have a deputy around here asking questions. You try and cooperate."

Shaw was still bobbing his head when Masters wheeled and boarded the elevator.

Evelyn Parks answered his knock by coming to the door herself. She had been dressing; she wore a robe and her hair was partly dressed. She stood aside to let him enter. Masters, at her invitation, sat down in the one chair; she herself sat on the side of the bed.

"You aren't doing me any good, coming up here," she said. "I've done all I could for you about that Carter business. I'd just as soon you stopped bothering me."

Masters smiled. "You talk pretty tough," he said. "It

ought to convince me but it doesn't. I brought you
some news. I'm going to make charges against George
Cox."

Her eyes showed interest tinged with a sudden
wariness. "Cox? What is this—some sort of a trick?
He's a cop. You're a cop. Cops don't arrest cops."

Masters said softly, "Sometimes they do, Evelyn. Cox
is getting money from you, isn't he?"

She looked up, meeting his gaze squarely. "When I
was a kid we believed in a lot of things. Santa Claus.
The Easter Bunny. And we were taught that if you
ever got lost or in trouble, all you had to do was go to
a cop. I learned about Santa Claus when I was seven
years old. I learned about cops when I was sixteen—
in the back of a station house. Maybe you're different.
I don't know, but it's a chance I have to take. We can
quit playing games, Sheriff. I mean about me being a
lady. We both know what I am. This is an old-fashioned
city, not New York or New Orleans. But it's not so old-
fashioned that people like me can get away with what
we do for a living. We have to pay for the privilege.
The Carter kid wouldn't pay."

Masters said gently, "And you think that that's why
she was killed?"

She shrugged. "You know a better reason? Have you
got a cigarette?"

When Masters mutely held up his pipe she said,
"Never mind. I've got a couple in my purse." She found
one and Masters lit it for her before she continued:

"I would have come to you anyway, even if you hadn't
come here. You don't have to believe that but I would
have. That fat bastard was shaking all of us down—
and that isn't all I could tell you about him."

Masters said nothing. This was her story. She would
tell it in her own way and in her own time.

"It was nothing new. Not to me anyway. He used to

come into this trap two or three times a week. He watched the girls. If they were hustlers—and he could tell—sooner or later he'd walk up and want to borrow five bucks. Never any more, never any less. Even a new girl would give him the money rather than take a ride downtown with him because even a new girl would know that he was the law. The girls that had been around here awhile would tip her off. Then the next week it would be another five." She snubbed her cigarette out viciously.

Masters felt anger rising inside him. He had not been greatly surprised, he remembered, at Benny Zurich's accusation of Cox. Cox, in his own way, was like Benny; like Joachim Carter. Each, after his fashion, preyed on women. Carter for degrading labor without even the recompense of occasional kindness. Benny Zurich for a dreary attraction for his dive. George Cox, presumably, for money. Each was vicious; each had a streak of pure animal. And each had preyed on Lucy Carter. He asked dourly, "Who else was in on it with him?"

Evelyn shrugged again. "Who knows? Maybe it was his own private racket. He didn't have anything to worry about. If you wanted to work, you paid him off. What he did with the money or how he split it was his business. If we complained—who would believe us?"

"You said he 'used' to come in here two or three times a week. Does that mean he stopped coming in?"

"About a week ago. The Carter kid had something to do with it. I told you she quit Benny's place about two weeks ago and started hanging around here all the time. She'd been living here for three months and she knew all about Cox. About a week or ten days ago we were sitting around, her and myself and another girl. The other girl was sore because Cox had been shaking her down and she was trying to get enough money together to go to Florida. Lucy laughed and said, 'That ape! He won't get a nickel from me!'"

"Did she say anything more about it?"

Evelyn shook her head. "She was pretty close-mouthed. It's easy to figure out, though. She had something on him. Sure enough, a day or so later he tried to borrow his usual five bucks from her and she laughed in his face. She talked to him a couple of minutes and he left and he hasn't been back since. We all tried to get her to tell us what she had on him but she wouldn't say what it was."

"What was Cox's reaction when she laughed at him?"

"At first he got red in the face. I thought he was going to hit her. He's good at that. She kept talking to him and he suddenly quit."

Evelyn stood up with considerable dignity. "That's all I know, Sheriff. You'd better go now. You're not doing my reputation any good."

Masters reached for a bill and her face flushed. "You don't have to do that."

Masters put the bill on the table. "The county pays a fee for witness service. You've got it coming for identifying the Carter girl if for nothing else."

The round-shouldered clerk scurried out from behind the desk when Masters emerged from the elevator into the lobby. "Sheriff," he said, the words coming hurriedly in his effort to please and conciliate Masters, "I thought of something you might want to know."

Masters waited, not speaking.

"About a week or so ago there was a man here looking for Lucy Carter. An old man. Sixty, maybe. Real tall—taller than you, and skinny. A mean-looking guy. He stopped at the desk and asked if she was registered here. I told him we had a Lucy Carter and he asked what room she had. I told him, but he didn't go up. He sort of grunted and walked away."

Masters recalled Joachim Carter as he had seen him earlier in the day. Tall—thin—most certainly a mean face. "Come upstairs with me," he said brusquely.

Three minutes later Ernest Shaw was looking at the photograph on Lucy Carter's dresser. "Sure," he said, positively, "That's him."

Masters called Tom Danning from the lobby. "I'll be at Chief Trowbridge's office," he said. He drove the few blocks to the city hall at no great speed, his mind occupied with planning his actions with regard to George Cox. Cox was tough and hard. He would not break up on the accusations of a known bad character such as Benny Zurich or a woman with a reputation like Evelyn Parks'. Given time to think he would realize that Benny Zurich would hardly swear to any information he might have given Masters.

Masters decided to hold back the identity of his informers and try to stampede the detective on the basis of a few unsupported accusations. If he had guilty knowledge of the Carter girl's murder he might be prone to panic. Masters realized that he could think of George Cox as a potential murderer with no great difficulty.

Big Trucks and his partner, Kirby, were lounging in the dingy anteroom to Trowbridge's office. Masters looked at the two detectives with a new interest born of the information he had received about their running mate, George Cox. If Cox was guilty of accepting bribes there was a reasonable likelihood that the other two were aware of it if not in collusion with him. The parallel could be traced further. If Cox had killed Lucy Carter because of a knowledge that she possessed— or to discipline the members of her group—there existed the possibility that these men knew of that too—or considered it a possibility.

He discounted the last thought to a degree. Of Kirby

he knew little. He had always considered Big Trucks to be an honest cop if a hard one. Watching their expressions, he saw nothing unusual. The usual dislike and nothing more. He felt some disappointment that George Cox was not present and knew a moment's worry that Benny Zurich might already have called, in which case Cox would now be covering up any tracks he might have left. Masters asked, "Is Chief Trowbridge in?"

Trucks said, "Yeah, Masters. Go on in."

Trowbridge, this time, made no pretense of being busy. He stood up and said fussily, "Oh. You. Hello, Masters—what can I do for you?"

Masters, having decided on a frontal attack, said curtly, "You can get George Cox in here while I ask him some questions."

Trowbridge reddened and his jaw dropped briefly before he swung to the attack. Like a banty rooster, Masters thought. Hackles lifted, eyes wild. "Now look here," he said in rising excitement, "you can't come in here with a request like that! By God, this is my department and I'll answer for any member of it!"

Masters asked quietly, "Up to and including shakedowns?"

Trowbridge sat down. "Shakedowns? Cox? That's insane!"

"This is how insane it is. If you don't produce him here where I can ask him some questions in the privacy of your office, I'll arrest him on sight myself and make formal charges."

Trowbridge said furiously, "And you'd do it, too, just to blacken the police department. By God, Masters—" The little chief came out from behind the desk and bustled to the door. He flung it open and shouted, "Trucks! Get George Cox—he's in the garage downstairs—and bring him in here! You too, Kirby. I want witnesses to this!"

Trowbridge had recovered some of his composure when George Cox shambled into the room with Kirby and Trucks a step behind him. He said angrily, "Sheriff Masters has made some remarks about you in connection with shakedowns, George. If you want to make a suit for slander I'll be glad to be a witness for you."

Cox wheeled toward Masters. "Why you hick sheriff," he rumbled, "I'll break your back!"

Masters stood his ground and fought back his own temper. It was vital to keep Cox infuriated now, give him no time to think. Cox hesitated. Trucks was staring at Masters with his peculiarly flat gaze. Kirby looked down at the floor, showing nothing. Trowbridge sat primly at his desk with his hands folded before him.

When it was obvious that Cox was coming no farther, Masters said, addressing Trowbridge but watching Cox, "Detective Cox has been taking money from women over on Water Street. I don't know how many—not yet. I know how much." He turned to Cox. "Five dollars a week apiece, wasn't it, George?"

Cox had started forward again at Masters' first words. The quotation of a figure checked him. It seemed to impress the other men in the room. Trucks transferred his flat stare to Cox, whose own eyes flickered from Masters to Trowbridge to Trucks and back again to Trowbridge. He licked his lips. "That's a damn lie, Chief," he said.

Masters said sardonically, "Don't waste your time and mine denying it, Cox. I'll produce witnesses when the time comes. You knew Lucy Carter, didn't you?"

Cox appealed to Trowbridge. "Do I have to stand here and listen to this?"

He had not denied knowing the dead girl. Masters,

needing the denial, pushed harder. "You approached the girl and tried to get money from her. She wouldn't pay. You couldn't have that, Cox. It might have given the other girls ideas. Did you kill her because of it?"

Cox shook his head as if to clear it. "I don't know who told you all this crap," he said, "but I'm going to find out. Some of those hustlers down on Water Street, I guess. Sure I know some of 'em. What would you expect? They're part of my job. But you'll play hell trying to show I ever took money from any of 'em, Masters, and I don't care who your witnesses are."

"Was Lucy Carter one of the ones you knew?" Masters persisted. He had dug the hole. Now it was up to George Cox.

Cox said, "No."

Masters dug the hole a little deeper. "You were never in her room?"

Cox appealed again to Trowbridge. "Do I have to listen to this? I already told him I didn't know the Carter kid."

Trowbridge's voice was faint. "You better answer him, George," he said.

"All right, God damn it. I didn't know her. I was never in her room. What more do you want?"

Masters said softly, "You're a liar. That's an old building, Cox and it's in poor shape. Even when you unlock the door to 304 you can't get in unless you know just how to lift up on the door. You were there with me yesterday morning. You opened the door for me without any hesitation."

Cox glanced from Trowbridge to Trucks. Seeking support, Masters thought, and not finding it. He shouted, "The hell with this. The hell with all of you!" and wheeled for the door.

Trowbridge called out sharply, "Trucks, stop him!"

Big Trucks stepped to one side to block Cox. Cox

halted for a space of perhaps a second and said harshly, "You big bastard, I always thought I could take you." With the words he swung a driving blow that took Trucks on the side of the neck. The bigger man did not flinch. He absorbed the blow and, pushing the frenzied Cox away with one hand, brought the other up in an open-handed cuff that landed on the side Cox's head. Cox, big as he was, shivered under the impact of the blow. Another cuff, and this time Trucks released his grip so that Cox spun backward, crashing into Trowbridge's desk and ricocheting from it to floor. A trickle of blood made a wandering path down his chin. He gathered both hands under him but made no effort to get up.

Trowbridge said hoarsely, "My God, Ed!" He scurried from behind his desk to stare down at Cox. "You fool," he said. "You dirty animal. Do you know what this is going to do to the department?" He turned back to Masters. "You think he killed her?"

Masters shrugged. "I don't know. He was afraid her. I'm going to make an investigation on my own hook, Trowbridge. I'm going to find out where he was Sunday night and what dealings he had with Lucy Carter. How you handle it is up to you. I'm ready arrest him right now on suspicion and take him with me—unless you want to book him here yourself. You might keep it quieter that way."

"I'll hold him," Trowbridge said bitterly. "What about it, George? Do you want to say anything?"

Cox lurched to his feet. "Not to you bastards," he mumbled.

Trucks put his hand on Cox's arm. Cox tried to shake it off but the grip was unbreakable and after a moment he stopped trying, seemed to shrink within himself.

"Oh, take him away," Trowbridge said.

Trucks asked, "What charge?"

Trowbridge thought for a moment. "Open," he said finally. "Hold him on an open count until we get a chance to check on where he was Sunday night."

Masters made arrangements to have Tom Danning present at the questioning of Cox and returned to his office. He gave the deputy instructions. "Sit in on the whole thing," he said. "Don't take anything for granted. How did Jake make out?"

Danning spread his hands in an indefinite gesture. "He talked to all the people Benny Zurich named. They'll all swear that Benny was at the Drive-In Sunday night. None of 'em will swear that he didn't leave at any given time."

"Let it go. Get on over to the police station now."

When Danning had left, Masters apologized to Bob Dunn. "One more phone call," he said, "and we'll go get something to eat."

The call was to Sheriff Sam Byrd in Simontown. "Sam," Masters said, "I've got a report down here that Joachim Carter may have been looking for Lucy a week or so ago. Could you look into it for me? I thought you might check the gas station where he buys his gas. He might have dropped a word. Don't go out to his place, though. I'd rather talk to Mrs. Carter first. And there's one other thing. His place is on an R.F.D. route, isn't it?"

Byrd agreed that it was.

"I doubt if he's the type that gets much mail. See if he got a letter a week or ten days ago. It would have been from Clay City. The R.F.D. carrier might just remember. Apparently Carter knew where to look for Lucy. I'd guess that she wrote to her mother and that he intercepted the letter."

On the other end of the wire Sam Byrd chuckled. "I'll see what I can do with the mail carrier, Ed. About the gas station—you're too long gone from the farm.

Carter buys his gas in fifty-gallon drums to get a break on the taxes. Buys it as tractor fuel."

Masters asked, "About that other business, the fact that she had a baby?"

Sam Byrd sounded apologetic. "I can't do anything there, Ed. I've talked to some of the young bucks, good and bad. They all claim they hardly knew the Carter girl."

Masters hung up with a feeling of impatient frustration. It was bad enough to have leads come to dead end. It was worse when they did not end but rather thinned and diverged. He said disgustedly, "The hell with it Bob. Let's go out and eat."

CHAPTER SEVEN

The two men ate at a restaurant a block from the courthouse. They were finishing their meal when the waitress approached to tell the sheriff that there was a telephone call for him.

Tom Danning was on the wire; his voice was shaking with anger. "They let him go, Ed," he said, repeating the words twice. "They let him go."

Masters hung up without waiting for further information. He signaled to Bob Dunn and the two men drove to the city hall, Masters explaining what had happened on the way.

Trowbridge was waiting for them in his office. Danning and Trucks were seated against the wall. Trowbridge got up as they came in and strode toward them. He was on the defensive, Masters thought. Trying to take the play away.

"Now before you say anything at all, Masters, I want you to listen to me. I know what you're going to say and I demand that you hear me out."

Masters stopped in front of Trowbridge's desk; Bob Dunn ranged up beside him. "I'll hear you," he said bitterly.

"I had Cox on an open charge. You were here at the time and you heard what I told Trucks. He demanded to see his lawyer as soon as we had him booked. I couldn't refuse. The lawyer got a writ of habeas corpus from Judge Fennelly. Now I wouldn't have let it go at that if I thought he was involved in the Carter murder, but Cox had an alibi for Sunday night. He told us about it—your deputy heard it. All we have to charge him with is conduct unbecoming a police officer and I've only got your say-so on that. If what you said is true we can handle it just as well on a departments basis."

"You sit there," Masters said, his voice cold with fury, "and tell me that one of your officers takes bribes to permit prostitution in his district and you're going to let him off with a departmental trial and possibly demotion?"

"He didn't admit to taking bribes."

"I told you I could produce witnesses. His hitting Trucks and trying to run out was admission in itself, Trowbridge."

"He lost his head," Trowbridge persisted. "He was a good officer once, Ed. He deserves another chance. He won't get off easy."

Masters shook his head. "You're damn right he won't get off easy. I'm going to take this thing to the attorney general and I'm going to have him picked up on sight by my people. Tell me about his alibi."

"They held a sports night at the Elks Club Sunday night. Cox was there. I talked to some of the men that attended the affair; Mayor Peters, for one. George Cox was positively present when the thing got under way and he was there when it broke up."

Masters said contemptuously, "I read some blurbs about that affair in the paper. They showed movies of the World Series. There were close to two hundred men present in a building that normally accommodates one hundred and fifty. You're a police officer. You know damn well that isn't an alibi. If Cox was noticed before it got under way and after it was over, in that mob, it was because he wanted to be noticed. Do you know who he sat with? Who he spent most of his time with?"

Trowbridge shook his head.

Masters continued: "You're in trouble, Trowbridge. I gave you evidence that points to Cox as a bribe-taker and possibly a murderer. To protect your department as much as possible from some bad publicity I let you hold him. If you couldn't hold him on the charge you had on the books you could have made additional charges that would have stuck. All you could see was a black mark against your department and you jumped at the chance for a whitewash."

Trowbridge set his jaw. "You're talking big, Masters," he said angrily. "All you have against Cox is that shakedown business and I don't know why I should have to take your word on even that. Cox isn't going anywhere. I can have him picked up in twenty minutes if you're going to make an issue of this."

Masters said, "You do that. You do just that." He turned to Tom Danning. "Tom," he said, "I don't understand why you didn't call me the minute Cox's lawyer showed up with that paper."

Danning looked angry and embarrassed. "I tried, Ed," he said. He jerked his head angrily toward Trucks. "Trucks wouldn't let me get to a telephone or a door. He wanted to give Cox a chance to get a lead. Then I wasted time calling Mrs. Lafferty's place. She told me you were at the restaurant."

Masters glanced at Trucks. "Did he put a hand on you?"

Danning answered ruefully. "I wish he had. No, he crowded me, blocked me."

Masters turned back to Trowbridge. "You let him out," he said flatly. "Now find him. And you'd better forget any plans you may have for holding him on an open charge and keeping this thing in the family."

Bob Dunn spoke for the first time since entering the room. "Do you have any idea where he was going?" he asked Trowbridge.

Trowbridge shook his head. "I don't know—unless he was going home."

Masters said, "Come on, Bob—Tom," and left the room.

In the car Tom Danning was apologetic. "I couldn't do a thing, Ed. Trowbridge had him on an open charge and the lawyer got a writ on the grounds of unlawful detention. Trowbridge could have fought it or he could have preferred another charge, but Cox kept needling him about how much better it would be to keep it hushed up."

"Let it go," Masters said. "We'll get him."

He parked the car in front of the courthouse. The leaden skies split open and a furious, pelting rain started to fall as they dashed for the shelter of the building. The first huge drops seemed to sizzle as they hit the warm pavement. Masters, inside the office, fumbled in a closet for his slicker and emerged to see Charlie Hess enter the room. The reporter had on a black raincoat that glistened in the electric light. Masters said, "Hello, Charlie. Thought you'd be out courting this time of the evening."

Hess took his rain hat off and slapped it against his leg. "Just heard about George Cox," he said. "You going after him?"

Masters nodded.

"He could have done it, Ed. Thinking about it, he could have done it."

"Chief Trowbridge didn't think so. He turned him loose."

Hess sat down but got up after a moment and began to pace the floor nervously. "He could have done it just the same. George is a queer sort of man, Ed. I knew him pretty well. He had a lot of pride. If he thought the Carter girl was going to expose him and ruin him he wouldn't have hesitated to kill her."

Bob Dunn asked curiously, "Pride? A corrupt cop who took money from prostitutes?"

Masters said, "I know what Charlie means. Tell him, Charlie." He watched the reporter thoughtfully as he spoke.

"You'd understand better if you knew where he lives," Hess explained to Dunn. "A big old mansion outside of town. Twenty rooms at least and he lives there all alone. His family had money once—lots of it—but they weren't new-rich. There have been Coxes in Clay City since the town was settled. George's father played with cotton futures and he got burned—lost everything but the house and then committed suicide. George was sixteen then. All his life he'd had everything. All of a sudden he had nothing but the house. He stayed on there with his mother until she died, then went into the army as a private. He didn't try for a commission. He stayed a private and he spent the war in a supply depot out on the West Coast. Then he came back here and got a job as a patrolman. You're a police officer yourself, Lieutenant Dunn. It's a good job and a necessary one. But for George Cox it was a comedown—very much of a comedown. He had offers. For old time's sake—call it noblesse oblige—some of the old family friends would have given him a job more in keeping with what he had been used to. He would have nothing to do with them. He seemed to take a perverse sort of pride in being humble to his old friends when he'd meet them—in a sardonic sort of way. Finally he had none left—and he made no new ones."

Danning nodded. "That's George," he said. "He kept the old place. I used to wonder how he kept up the taxes on it. I guess we know now."

Hess continued: "Trowbridge made him a detective after a couple of years. It didn't change him."

Masters had finished putting on his slicker. He looked at Dunn. "I'd like to take you along with me," he said doubtfully. "It's probably going to keep right on raining and you don't have a raincoat."

Hess said, "I've got one in the back of my car he can take, Ed. It's an old one I use when I go fishing." Without waiting for an answer he left the room, returning after a few moments with a yellow oilskin which he handed to Dunn. Dunn separated the stiff folds of the slicker and slipped his hands into the sleeves.

Masters slipped his pistol under the waistband of trousers, beneath the sheltering folds of the slicker. "Tom," he said, "you take downtown. Lieutenant Dunn and I will go on out to Cox's house. Trowbridge won't be making more than a gesture at finding Cox." He turned to Charlie Hess. "You want to come along?"

The reporter shook his head. "I'd like to, Ed, but I've got things to do." He turned to leave the room.

Masters watched his retreating back and then turned to Dunn. "You ready?" he asked.

CHAPTER EIGHT

It had been comparatively easy to make a fool of Trowbridge—a fool to begin with. There had been the strong weapon of publicity: a black mark against the Department. There had been the open charge, a charge that was effective for no longer than it took a prisoner to reach a lawyer. George Cox, walking from the detention cells to the parking lot behind the police station, did not make the mistake of assuming that Ed Masters was a fool. He got into his car, an old black sedan and the biggest model that its maker produced. Too big, really. A car designed for the care of a chauffeur. Now it was shabby and poorly kept.

There was that Parks woman. He had to get to her before Masters found out that he had been released and came after him. It had to be her who had talked to the sheriff. There were dozens like her down on Water Street, but he knew Masters had talked to her and he was sure it had been her. He stepped on the starter. The battery ground sluggishly before the motor caught in a ragged spasm of coughing. Yes, it had been Evelyn Parks and if an object lesson was made of her, Masters would play hell trying to find another witness. He had made a mistake on the Carter business and he knew it now. Water over the dam, but he should not have denied knowing her. It would have made no difference. Benny. He would have to call him, too, and tell him to keep his mouth shut. He knew Benny Zurich. Like the other wolves. If he started to trip and go down, they would all turn on him.

The rain was coming down harder. This would be a real gully-washer, and already the windshield wipers, trying to steal compression vacuum from the worn cylinders, were swamped. He felt the need of a drink. He had to think and these days thinking came hard.

He steered between the two stone pillars that flanked the driveway leading up to the big house that had been his father's and his father's father's. In the weak glare of the headlights it loomed before him like some monstrous ark, brooding and ugly. He stopped the car under the overhang of the porte-cochere and walked up the sagging steps. In his own memory the two carriage lamps that hung on either side of the door would have been lit by sundown. There would have been a servant to open the door that he now unlocked and pushed back himself. He did not turn on the hall light; instead he pushed on through to the library that had been his father's and turned on the rococo wrought-iron chandelier that held four naked bulbs. He could not wait here too long. Masters would be coming.

Cox stripped off his damp suitcoat and walked to the study table. There was a gallon jug half full of clear liquor on the table, stoppered with a twist of waxed paper. He found a murky glass, poured it half full of liquor and drank it down, shuddering spasmodically. Corn. Lousy corn whisky. Moonshine. His father had called it a stable drink and would have none of it in the house. He refilled his glass. Have to be careful now. Not take too long thinking. He flung himself into a leather Morris chair, legs outstretched, his unshaven chin sunk on his chest.

The rain drummed on the roof two stories above. Came through the roof, he knew, in some of the back rooms. Never had been enough money to have it fixed. Never would be, probably, but think now. About this jam. If he saw the Parks girl alone, talked to her, he could probably scare her into keeping her mouth shut. He closed his right hand into a fist and slapped it into open palm of the other hand. What he'd like to do. And the Carter murder. Masters had been smart there. Getting him to deny that he had ever been in the little broad's room and then bringing out that business about the door. That was when you panicked, George, he told himself. He could have been in the room before she rented it, for all Masters knew. He had been there, all right.

"I know all about you and your five-dollar loans," Lucy Carter had said. That had been in the bar and there had been people around. "I wouldn't give you a dime."

He had wanted to slap her. Little slut. "Get your coat," he had threatened. "We'll take a little ride and see if you want to change your mind." He had almost hoped that she would still refuse so that he could get her into the car. No people around then.

She had laughed. If she had just defied him he could have handled her. He had done it before and he could do it again, but the laugh had an edge of contempt that had puzzled him, unbalanced him.

The glass was empty again. He got up to fill it.

"If I take a ride with you," she had said, "you'll be sorrier about it than I will. You still want me to go with you?"

Her confidence made him uneasy. "Let it go," he had growled. "I'll talk to you later. What's your room number?"

He drank again from the glass, shuddering again. He had to remember that he must get out of here before Masters came.

He got up and walked unsteadily across the room. There was a portrait on the far wall of an austere man in his middle years. A thin, ascetic face. "Four hundred bucks," he mused. He stood, heavy legs wide apart, staring at the picture. If this man had considered drinking moonshine to be vulgar, what would he have thought of his son being arrested on charges of taking money from whores? Cox smiled. The opinion of a man who had killed himself shouldn't matter. He had disqualified himself from having opinions at the moment he had blown his brains out with a shotgun, leaving wife and son to face the pity of his friends.

Pity. He had had none of it. After the war, when he had put on the uniform of a patrolman, they had sucked around, gratifying their curiosity. Showing him that they were democratic about it all. The hell with them.

Have to get out of here before long. He swallowed another mouthful of the strong liquor. Had to get to Evelyn Parks and make her keep her mouth shut. And the Carter thing. Not much he could do there unless he wanted to tell what had happened when he went to her room, and he wasn't quite ready to do that. Not yet.

He had followed her there, catching up with her in the hall.

"You," she had said without interest and without fear. "Come in. Lift up on the door—it sticks." She had crossed the room to sit on the edge of the bed.

He had tried to intimidate her. "What's this crap about my being sorry if I take you down to the station?"

She had laughed again. "You want to try it and find out?"

He had moved forward, one fist clenched. "You little slut. Who do you think you're talking to?"

She hadn't been afraid; she had stood up to face him. "I'm not scared of you," she had said. "If I told a certain person about you they'd run you out of town."

That had stopped him. "Go on," he had said, trying

to make it sound ominous. "What certain person?"

She had been clever enough to realize that her own threat was more menacing if she kept him guessing. "Take me in and find out," she had mocked him.

He hadn't been able to bring himself to do it even though he was aware of the danger in letting himself be backed off by this girl. Now he wished he had, regardless of the risk that she might know somebody important enough to make trouble for him. Threats and wheedling hadn't gotten the name of that somebody, and he had backed away like a dog puzzled when his barkings and growlings are ignored, telling himself that he would play it safe until he found out what it was that gave this girl the guts to defy him.

He sank back in the Morris chair again. Some instinct worked inside him. He had been a cop for nearly ten years and you didn't spend that much time without picking up a feeling for crime and criminals. He had sat in this very room, in this very chair, for many hours, thinking about the Carter girl and who it was that she knew who could hurt him. He had spent additional hours of his off-duty time watching her, trying to determine which of the men she spoke to, drank with, danced with, went upstairs with, was, in her mind, big enough to go up against him. Now he thought about the unknown person in terms of murder rather than as a threat to George Cox. If a whore turned to you for protection, she had to be deeply involved with you, and you with her, and involvement with a whore had motivated more than one murder. He was sure now he could work it out given time— but there was no time. Masters would be coming for him as soon as he learned of his release. He stood up. There was a place. It was already too late to go to the Oceanus House to see Evelyn Parks. Masters would think of that and have a man downtown. So he would go to Benny's. He started for the door, paused and went back for the jug of whisky.

Once started, he was impatient to be out of this house. He swore when the old car didn't start immediately. When it did start he swung almost viciously from the driveway to the highway, blinded by the dripping rain that shattered into thousands of tiny points of light on the windshield.

He had to make a call first. A drugstore wouldn't do. Too many people. He swung the big old car in at a gas station and got out, leaving the motor running and waving the attendant back when he would have come out. "Telephone," he explained, reaching into his pocket for change.

He called Benny's Drive-In, getting Benny after a minute or two. "This is Cox," he said. "I'll be out." He hung up immediately, not waiting for any reply. The attendant had gone out when he turned away from the phone. He thought for a moment and turned back, fumbling for another coin.

When he asked for the second number the operator said, "Wait one moment please," and after a moment: "Were you calling the sheriff's office?" He mumbled that he was.

"Sheriff Masters is out," she said. "If you leave your number I will have him call you when he returns."

Cox was familiar with this routine that Masters, lacking a night deputy, had established. He started to shake his head, realized what he was doing and said, "Let it go." After a pause he added, "Tell him that Detective George Cox called," and hung up, wondering why he had bothered to identify himself by rank and smiling as he realized that after all these years he was still playing the part of a cop.

He was not particularly disappointed that he had not been able to reach Masters. Now that he thought about it, calling the sheriff had been a futile thing to do. George Cox was going under anyway. Chief Trowbridge would make him the goat for everything that had gone wrong with the department in the last five years.

Except that it would be a pretty clever thing, letting Masters know that the Carter kid had a connection of some kind. Masters was smart enough to work it out and that would be a sort of a horse laugh on Trowbridge. Also it might take some of the pressure off him—put Masters onto a new and hotter suspect.

He drove off in a clattering of worn gears.

A second car had driven into the filling station behind Cox's. The attendant, coming from some errand behind the station, waved a hand to indicate he would be there in a minute and stepped into the station. When he came out again the second car was pulling out after Cox's car. The attendant, mumbling something about damn fools who couldn't wait for five seconds, hoped out loud that the damn fool in question would run out of gas.

George Cox drove rapidly for the Drive-In, wanting another drink badly now. He did not pull in on the black-top parking area; instead he drove up a service road that ended in a lattice-bordered cul-de-sac that hid a row of garbage and trash cans from the trade. He got out of the car, taking the jug with him, and lumbered through the wet to one of a line of cabins. Inside he pulled down the shade before he turned on the light.

He could think now. Masters would have his deputies out looking for him, but they would probably be satisfied with checking the Drive-In itself. Damn few people knew about him and this cabin. Thinking about it, he was ashamed of the moment of weakness that had led him to call the sheriff. He lay down on the sagging bed, arms pillowing his head. The gun that he carried in his leather-lined hip pocket bothered him, pressing uncomfortably against his buttocks. He reached for it and put it on the night table, pouring himself a drink at the same time. He drank the better part of it and lay back again. This time the light hurt his eyes. He got up and turned it out. When, an hour later, his visitor came, Cox was almost unconscious. He came awake as some hard object was being inserted in his mouth; he tried to bite down on it, to thrust it out with his tongue. When it raked cruelly against his palate he tried to cry out even as he realized, too late, what it was.

CHAPTER NINE

Masters returned to the courthouse briefly with Bob Dunn shortly after eleven o'clock. The telephone was whirring even as the two men walked into the office. Masters took the call; it was the operator, reporting George Cox's attempted call. Having reported it, the operator, on the point of closing the circuit, said, "Here's another call, Sheriff Masters."

Benny Zurich identified himself, his voice taut. "You better get out here, Masters," he said. "George Cox has killed himself in one of my cabins."

Danning had had the assignment of checking Zurich's place earlier in the hunt for Cox. He had reported to Masters that Cox was not there, had not been there and that his car was not in the parking space.

Masters hung up and turned to Dunn. He explained what had happened and made quick arrangements for Dunn to get the coroner and to try and locate the two deputies and then to follow him out to the Drive-

In with the laboratory trailer.

The lights of Benny's place were still on, the blue and red neon tubes each having its own nimbus in the dying drizzle that was an aftermath of the earlier thundershowers. There were still a half-dozen cars in the parking lot when Masters drove the county car in and parked close to the main building. He got out of the car and walked in long strides to the entrance. The door was open and in the amber light of the room he could see a gaggle of people—perhaps ten—in the far corner of the room. He recognized Benny Zurich and Hazel King; the rest were strangers. The group was seated in a scattering of chairs pulled helter-skelter from adjoining tables. The group looked up as a unit when Master entered and Benny got to his feet. He wore a pair of tan slacks and a white shirt, open at the throat. He came toward Masters at a half trot, explaining as he came.

"He's out in one of the cabins, Sheriff. The poor bastard blew half his head off."

"What time did he check in here?"

Hazel King had come up behind Benny. She answered Masters' question before Benny could speak. "He didn't," she said. "We didn't even know he was there."

Masters glanced at her briefly. She had come a long way in a short time. You could measure her progress by her choice of pronouns. Given time and it would be I not we, if she didn't lose her grip on Benny. "You'll sure it's Cox?" he asked.

Benny nodded his head. "I know him pretty well," he said. "He used to hang around here a lot. It's Cox."

They had been moving steadily toward the larger group that remained at the tables. Masters said to the group, "You people stay right here." He said over his shoulder to Benny, "You come along and show me where it is."

The two men walked through the drizzle to the last cabin in a row of half a dozen. The light had been left on inside. Masters said, "You get on back," to Benny and pushed on the flimsy door of the cabin. It swung open at his touch and he stepped inside.

The body of George Cox lay face upward on the bed. The sheets had been twisted away from the mattress so that the rusty marks left by the iron springs showed in a waffle pattern. Cox was fully dressed except for his shoes; these had been kicked off and lay beside the bed. His arms were outflung and his legs were in a bicyclist's posture, one outthrust and one doubled up. The bullet had entered through the roof of his mouth and emerged at the top of his skull in an ugly gush of blood, bone splinters and brain tissue. Where the skin was not covered with dark blood his face was a livid gray and oddly shrunken. Stepping carefully into the room, Masters could see a short-barreled revolver on the floor where it had apparently dropped from Cox's relaxing hand. Beside the bed stood a gallon jug and an empty glass. There was a smell of alcohol in the musty little room mingled with the rank, peppery bite of exploded gunpowder and the sick-sweet smell of blood.

There was only the one door to the room. No bathroom. Occupants, then, had to use the outhouse. There was running water. A tiny basin filled one corner of the room. There was only a cold-water tap; where the hot-water tap should have been there was a round hole in the back of the basin.

Masters stepped outside, closing the door softly behind him. The rain had almost completely stopped. He took a flashlight from his pocket and bent down, throwing the beam of light at an angle across the grass in front of the cabin. The Bermuda grass was tough and springy. It showed no trace even of his or Benny's recent tracks. He stepped to the corner of the building. There was a late-model black coupe pulled in to shelter between Cox's and the adjacent cabin. It had Florida plates. He flashed the light on the steering post and read the name on the registration certificate. Theodore Harrison. Masters made a note of the name and the address typed below it before he headed back to the main building.

The group of frightened people were sitting in almost the same positions they had occupied when he had left the room: Three waitresses in white uniforms (on this rainy night the carhops would have been sent home early). Two men in denims and T-shirts, half drunk and getting over it rapidly. Two other women, unclassified, one of them apparently the companion of a fat little man in a gaudy sport shirt and flannel trouser that fitted his pudgy legs too tightly. Benny and Hazel King.

Masters asked, "Who found him?"

The fat little man in the sport shirt started to get up changed his mind and sat down again. From his seat he said tremulously, "I did. My God, it was terrible!"

Masters asked, "You're Theodore Harrison?" and was mildly pleased when the fat man nodded his head even as his eyes opened in a combination of surprise and fright.

The fat man's companion was at least fifteen years younger than he and there was some malice in Masters' next question. "Is this your wife?"

Harrison shook his head mutely.

Masters sat down, pushing aside a clutter of bottles and ash trays. "Tell me about it," he said easily. "Start with the time you registered."

Benny started to speak and Masters gestured impatiently. Harrison stammered for a moment before he could get the words out. "Nine o'clock," he said finally. "I was driving up from St. Augustine. I saw the lights here and decided to stop for the night instead of going in to Clay City. I met this young lady and we had a few drinks."

Masters said, "That's an expensive car you've got out there. Do you make a practice of staying in roadside cabins that have outside plumbing?"

Harrison bit his fat lower lip and Masters relented. "What time did you get to your cabin?"

Harrison said eagerly, "Ten-thirty." He reddened. "The young lady came along with me to have a nightcap."

"What time did you hear the shot?"

Harrison looked puzzled. "I didn't hear a shot."

"Then how did you happen to find the body?"

Harrison straightened a little and set his pursy jaw. "I can explain that," he said. "I had to go to the bathroom. The—place—is at the end of the line of buildings. It was dark outside and I had the flashlight from the dashboard of my car. When I came back I walked into the wrong cabin."

"Was the light on?"

Harrison shook his head. "If it was I wouldn't have walked into it. I had turned the light out in my cabin before I opened the door. The young lady asked me to so nobody would see her in there. I had the light in my hand and I flashed it ahead of me so I wouldn't trip on the furniture, and I saw it. I told the young lady and we came and told the manager."

Benny spoke up. This time Masters let him continue. "He came back and told me," he said. "Just like he said he did. It was just a couple of minutes before eleven. I called your office right away." His voice took on a belligerent edge. "Now look, Sheriff. The guy killed himself. Anybody can see that. What's the use of holding all these people here? They don't know anything about it."

Masters said, "I'll be the judge of that." He would have continued but he was interrupted by the squeal of brakes outside the door. Bob Dunn came in followed by Jake Bowen and the coroner, Doc Adams. Masters went forward to meet them out of earshot of the people at the table.

"Where is he, Ed?" Doc Adams asked tiredly.

Masters told him and the coroner left with Bob Dunn on his heels. Masters, when they had gone, drew Jake Bowen aside. "Where's Tom Danning?" he asked.

"I thought there would be enough of us here," Bowen said. "I told him to go on in to the office. Want me to call him?"

"Let it go. Talk to these people here. Find out if anyone heard a shot. I doubt if they did. They probably had the juke box going full blast. And we'll take Benny back to town with us when we're through."

Doc Adams was finished with the body of George Cox when Masters again entered the cabin. He was bent over his instrument case, putting his gear away, and Bob Dunn was moving in with tape measure and camera. Adams straightened up. "No question about this one, Ed. Death due to massive hemorrhage and radical destruction of brain tissue. In short, a bullet through the head. Had the gun in his mouth when he pulled the trigger. Happened, I'd say, close to two hours ago."

Masters asked quickly, "How accurate would that be, Doc?"

Adams shrugged. "A little hard to say. The heat in this place would make a difference. Within twenty minutes, maybe. That would put it somewhere between nine-fifteen and nine forty-five. You'll have to get me another jury."

Bob Dunn took several pictures, the flare of the flash bulbs making white lightning within the drab room. He put down the camera and said, "Let me have a match, Ed."

Masters gave him a packet. Dunn opened a black case and took out an aluminum pan and an alcohol lamp. He crumbled bits of a waxy, granular material into the pan and lit the lamp beneath it.

Doc Adams, watching with bored interest, asked, "Paraffin test?"

Dunn smiled. "That's what the fact-detective magazines call it. Actually it's the Lunge Reaction Test. It's not too accurate most of the time but it has its uses. We're lucky in this case." He gestured toward the body of Cox. "His gun was old and pretty badly worn. You get a heavy blowback in the web of the thumb from a cheap or worn revolver or from some automatics. I'll be able to tell you with reasonable certainty whether or not Cox fired a gun immediately before he died."

He had been melting the wax over the lamp. Now he walked toward the bed and picked up the limply dangling hand of George Cox. He dripped the wax slowly onto the wrist and the bases of thumb and forefinger. When he had a heavy coating he placed a square of gauze on the wax and poured a second layer. He turned to face Masters, still holding the dead hand. "I'll wash this cast with diphenylamine," he said. "The nitrate in the gunpowder, if any, will turn blue in the reaction." He added wistfully, "The hell of it is that tobacco, urine and some detergents will also give a positive reaction."

There was a knock on the door of the cabin. Masters said, "Come on in," and Charlie Hess entered. He looked at the bed and almost as quickly looked away.

"I'm almost sorry for the poor devil," he said.

"Trowbridge is on his way out," he continued to Masters. He winked theatrically. "Somebody telephoned in to his duty sergeant. The sergeant called me before he called Trowbridge but don't tell him that." He grimaced. "Smells like a distillery in here."

Dunn had taken the now stiffened shell of wax from Cox's hand and rinsed it with a clear liquid from a glass container. He turned to Masters and held out the cast. The inside was flecked with particles of grayish blue. Dunn said, "I'd go on record, Ed. He fired a gun. This reaction is almost a classic example."

Doc Adams grunted. "I could have told you that. You didn't think somebody else stuck the barrel of that pistol in his mouth, did you? Or that he lay there and let them do it?"

Masters said doubtfully, "I'm not so sure, Doc. He must have been pretty drunk. You can run a blood count and see just how drunk." He held out his hand. "Let me take that cast," he said.

He studied the cast carefully, holding it, for comparison, against his own right wrist. "You're the criminologist, Bob," he said. "Take a look at the formation of those powder particles. Heavy on the base of the thumb. Look close and you'll see a blank strip across the first joint of the thumb. If somebody put the gun in his hand and held it there, his thumb would have been shielded right where that blank is by the forefinger. I think you'll have to give it to me that somebody could have done that."

Dunn said skeptically, after looking again at the cast, "I'll admit it's a possibility, Ed. Nothing more than that. You can't predict particle formation."

Masters shook his head. "I can't see him committing suicide. If I could, I can't see him calling me before he did it. Trowbridge, maybe, or Trucks or one of his own people. Not me."

Hess asked quickly, "He called you? What did he say, Ed?"

Masters turned to face the reporter. "Why nothing at all, Charlie," he said. "He didn't get through to me."

Doc Adams said wearily, "Wish you'd get me my jury, Ed. I'm an old man and these night calls don't make me feel any younger."

Masters said, "Charlie, you're a county resident. You make one. I'll send Jake in and a couple of those people inside."

He walked into the main building to find Benny swearing in a high-pitched, angry voice. "You can ask me anything you want right here," he shouted. "God damn it, Masters," he appealed, catching sight of the sheriff, "this guy Bowen says I'm pinched!"

Masters asked placidly, "You didn't expect anything else, did you?"

Hazel King studied Masters closely and then put her hand on Benny's arm. "Better go along," she said. "I'll take care of things here."

The sheriff sent the two farmhands and one of the waitresses to report to the coroner. Jake Bowen briefed him. "That Harrison," he said, "I let him go. He called up and got a room at the Everett House. He'll be there when we want him. Nobody heard a shot."

Both men looked up at the wailing of a siren. That would be Trowbridge, Masters guessed. The siren was typical. In a moment Trowbridge bustled into the room, followed by a uniformed man. "Where's Cox?" he demanded and, without waiting for an answer: "My God, Masters. This is a terrible thing to happen. Did he leave a confession?"

"There wasn't one in the cabin," Masters told him.

It was close to two o'clock in the morning when Masters walked into his office again with Benny, Jake

Bowen and Bob Dunn in tow. Benny had relapsed into a sullen silence. The verdict of Doc Adams' jury had been "probable suicide." Dunn had questioned the "probable."

"The way I see it, Ed, he killed the Carter girl. Everything points to a strong motive and he knew that his alibi wouldn't stand up against an investigation, so he killed himself to clean the slate. Maybe he didn't intend to do it when he called your office. Still, from what Hess said, he was the morose type. The more he drank, the darker things got, so finally, there was only one answer, one solution."

Hess had agreed. "What the hell, Ed—what more proof do you want?"

Even Trowbridge, by implication, had conceded Cox's guilt in the Carter murder. Masters, weary now and dispirited, called for Benny Zurich. He was in no mood to be patient and he made it clear.

"Suicide or not," he said to Benny, "you've got a lot of dirt on your shoes. I don't believe there's any way you can make it easy on yourself as far as I'm concerned, but if I were you, I'd try. We'll start with Cox being in that cabin. He wasn't registered, according to your own statement."

Benny was seated in a wooden chair, his elbows on his knees, head in his hands. He said tonelessly, "Cox had a key to that cabin. He came out there sometimes; maybe once or twice a month. He'd have a woman with him or sometimes he'd come alone with a bottle. He always called me ahead of time so I wouldn't rent the cabin."

"Did he call you last night?"

"Yes. About eight o'clock. He didn't give me a chance to answer him; just said he was coming out."

"Did he pay for using the cabin?"

Benny laughed. "Like hell. I told you he was bleeding

me. Liquor, meals, the cabin—he never gave up a dime."

For another hour he denied any complicity in the Carter murder or any knowledge of George Cox's death. Masters then sent him down to the cells in charge of a yawning Tom Danning and went home with Dunn to get whatever sleep he could.

Tired as he was, he fretted, nevertheless, before he dropped full length on the feather mattress. For lack of a better charge, he had used "maintaining a public nuisance" as his basis for holding Zurich. The charge would hold no longer than it would take Zurich's attorney to get to Judge Fennelly's office in the morning, With the stink at the Drive-In, he had a better than fair chance of getting Benny's license. There was some satisfaction in that. It stuck in his mind that Zurich, knowing that Cox was in the cabin and probably drunk, could easily have slipped outside and shot him with his own gun. If Zurich, for instance, had killed the Carter girl and Cox suspected it and was using his knowledge to blackmail Zurich for money to get out of town.... The if was pretty big to hold a man on, he thought ruefully. Especially since Doc Adams and Bob Dunn were so damn sure that Cox had killed himself. Charlie Hess was sure it was suicide, too, he remembered, as he dropped into the black pit of sleep.

CHAPTER TEN

Masters had slept but little in spite of his weariness He was rather surly at breakfast with Bob Dunn. Dunn stated his plans cheerfully enough: "I hope to be getting out of here sometime this afternoon, Ed. I'll develop the pictures I took out at the cabin the first thing this morning. Give you a written report if you want one."

Masters nodded silently. Dissatisfaction with the obvious, the logical explanation of George Cox's suicide, rode heavily on his shoulders—if it was suicide. Mrs. Lafferty, coming in with a pot of coffee, commented on it. "Just because you're going to a funeral, Ed Masters, you don't have to act so much like it."

He glanced up and grinned at her, noticing that she was already dressed in a dark-blue street dress. "I'm going," she explained. "The way you talked about that poor child I feel as if it's my duty. Especially since the mother will be there."

The two hours that Masters spent in his office were busy enough. Benny's lawyer dropped in and arranged for a hearing for his client later in the week before a magistrate. In the meantime Benny had been freed on a nominal bail. Jake Bowen was already out trying to break down Zurich's alibi for Sunday night. Bowen hadn't liked the assignment. From the lackadaisical attitude he had worn when he started out Masters was certain that the deputy was satisfied that George Cox had killed the Carter girl and himself, but he had gone without argument. Charlie Hess dropped in.

"We're going to take the position that he killed himself out of remorse for having killed the Carter girl, Ed," he said. "Can I give that as your opinion?"

Masters shook his head. "I don't like to be stubborn," he said. "I'll admit that it would make a nice, clean package. But how are you going to explain the fact that he had an alibi for the time of her death?"

Hess grimaced. "That Elks Club thing? You said yourself it wasn't much of an alibi. You practically told Trowbridge as much. Has anything happened to make you change your mind?"

"No."

"Then why don't you accept the fact that he killed the girl?"

Masters studied Hess. "It isn't that I don't accept it, Charlie." He stood up. Hess had been breathing on his neck throughout this case. Now he was crowding a little too far, trying to put words in his mouth for the sake of a by-lined story, and the sheriff was irritated by it. "I've got to get moving," he said, glancing at his watch in a gesture of dismissal. "Mrs. Carter and Lucy's brother will be getting in for the funeral. There's a bus due in five minutes. I suppose they'll be on it. I don't think old Carter would let them take the car. Funeral is at eleven. You coming?"

Hess shook his head. "Too much to do."

Masters watched Hess leave, deliberately waiting a few seconds so he would not have to walk to the street with him. It was typical, he supposed. The Carter girl, newly murdered at the hands of an unknown person, was news. But now George Cox was news, and the girl had newspaper value only in terms of the fact that Cox had killed her—or so the *Inquirer* would imply.

The bus was five minutes late. Masters bought an Atlanta paper and sat down on a hard wooden bench to read it. There was nothing on Cox's suicide. If Charlie Hess had filed copy with the wire service it had been too late for the state edition.

Lucy Carter's mother and brother were on the bus. The woman wore a shapeless black dress and a close-fitting black hat. Her face was white and drawn. She had on a pair of black gloves, obviously new and as obviously inexpensive; as she got off the bus she flexed her fingers continually as if she were unused to wearing them. Probably wore them to hide her reddened, workworn hands, Masters thought, rather than as a badge of mourning and he felt real pity for the woman. The boy, Abel, followed his mother from the bus. He was scowling, eyebrows furrowed over a set mouth. As if, Masters thought, he had put the expression on in the morning as a defense against any sign of weakness. He wore a new and ill-fitting suit and new shoes. She would have had a time, the sheriff thought, in making her preparations. He doubted that Carter had advanced the money for the clothes. Maybe she had saved some or maybe the little storekeeper, Jim Dreyer, had helped. He walked forward to meet them and was aware of another hurrying figure beside him. He turned to see Martha Lafferty.

"Couldn't have that poor woman come down here all this way to bury her child and no woman to talk with," she said. "Ed, I'm going to take her out to the house to freshen up—her and the boy. And after the funeral she's to go back with me and stay till she's ready to go home. You make sure there's plenty of flowers and tell that Gregory I'll give him a piece of my mind if everything isn't done real nice."

Masters, greatly relieved, said, "You're a pretty good sport, Martha Lafferty."

She reddened and poked him with an elbow. "Nothing of the sort, Ed Masters. And you get them deputies of yours to come to the funeral. She don't have to know they're deputies."

Mrs. Carter had stepped from the bus to stand uncertainly looking about her. She recognized Masters as he approached. "I'm glad you met us, Sheriff," she said. "I didn't know just where to go."

Abel, still scowling, moved forward to stand protectively beside her. "We'd've been all right," he mumbled.

Martha Lafferty introduced herself and quickly took charge. The Carters and Martha were gone almost before he was aware of it, and her last instructions still hung in the air. "We'll be there right at eleven, Ed. You run along now and see that everything is all right."

He passed Martha's instructions along to Gregory, the undertaker, remembering also to hand him the five-dollar bill that Jim Dreyer had given him to buy flowers with and adding a bill of his own. Gregory, bustling about importantly, nodded his head. "Martha doesn't have to worry," he said. "This is a nice funeral. Everything looks lovely. Would you like to see the deceased?"

Masters, remembering the glade on the Kingsbridge Pike and Lucy Carter as he had seen her then, declined. Unbelievably he had a free half hour. He lit his pipe and strolled down a side street, avoiding the main avenue where he would have been halted for conversation a dozen times. Time to think now, to work over this uneasy conviction that George Cox's suicide was not the mathematically precise solution that Bob Dunn, for instance, thought it to be. Say that George Cox had killed himself in a fit of remorse. Masters, puffing deliberately, could not remember having seen any sign of remorse or the possibility of such an emotion in George Cox—or George Cox's type, for that matter. Say that fear of disgrace to what had been a good name had furnished the tension for his trigger finger. There was more disgrace in being a pimp than in being a murderer, and Cox had been kissing cousin to a pimp in soliciting money from prostitutes. The sheriff would have given a great deal to know, for instance, why Cox had tried to call him a few short hours before his death.

Masters wheeled and started back up the shady street down which he had wandered. He was anxious now to talk with the Carter woman just as soon as the funeral was over and it was decently possible. Anxious, too, for Sam Byrd's call with regard to any information he might have picked up from the R.F.D. carrier who might or might not have delivered a letter to Joachim Carter, and remembered it. Of course, it might well be wasted effort, empty conjecture—if you assumed that George Cox had killed the Carter girl and then blown his own brains out either from fear or remorse. Dunn figured it that way but Dunn had the objective mind of the scientist, trained to deal with probabilities and the neat equations of chemical and physical fact, not the muddled, unbalanced swirl of human behavior.

Supposing you assumed that Cox's death was a homicide. Masters frowned, then grinned. Do that and you could suspect just about the whole of Clay County. He increased his pace. Time to get back for the funeral. Not the whole of Clay County though, he reflected. He remembered Benny Zurich's statement of two days ago: "Lucy Carter knew something or somebody. She could have ruined George Cox in this town." Something could not be isolated now. Whoever had killed Lucy Carter had accomplished that. If it were "somebody"—that was something else again. Not too many people in Clay County were important enough to bother Cox.

There was a respectable gathering at the funeral. Besides the Carters there were Martha Lafferty and a dozen of her friends—dragooned, Masters supposed, for the occasion. Jake Bowen—when he saw Masters he shook his head and raised his shoulders in a gesture of futility. He hadn't been able, apparently, to shake Benny Zurich's Sunday night alibi. Tom Danning. Bob Dunn. Gregory the undertaker had sent a delegation. And Evelyn Parks. Without makeup she looked younger than Masters remembered her. The ceremony was short. The clergyman provided by Gregory intoned the traditional words and it was over. Masters saved his attention for the Carters. Mrs. Carter shed no tears. Her face was white—whiter than it had been when she arrived on the bus—but it showed no trace of emotion. Abel Carter came closer to breaking. Masters, watching, saw his mouth working as he tried to keep his control. His admiration for Mrs. Carter increased. There was iron in this woman.

The gathering broke up swiftly. Masters sought out Martha Lafferty. "I've got to stop at the office for a few minutes," he said. "I'll be on out in a little bit. I want to talk to Mrs. Carter and the boy."

She agreed and bustled off to shepherd Mrs. Carter and the boy into her old coupe. Masters returned to his office and called the Everett House, asking specifically for Theodore Harrison, the fat little man who had discovered George Cox's body.

Harrison, when the connection was made, said nervously, "Hello, Sheriff. I've been waiting to hear from you."

Masters smiled. The fat little man had had enough law to last him for a time. "You can leave now," he said officiously. "Be a good idea to stick to hotels."

Harrison agreed effusively. Masters hung up and went out to the car for his trip to Mrs. Lafferty's house.

For all her tact, Martha Lafferty had been unable to put Mrs. Carter or her son at ease. They sat stiffly in her best room. Mrs. Carter clutched her pocketbook tightly in her gloved hands; the boy had his big hands folded in the classic schoolboy position. When Masters entered the room, Martha Lafferty rose from her own chair. "I'll make some coffee," she said.

Masters sat down and lit his pipe, taking his time. The Carters, mother and son, stared at him silently. He began, "Mrs. Carter, how long had your daughter been gone from home?"

She paused for thought and said finally, "Fourteen months."

"And you had no word from her in all that time?"

Abel said sullenly, "We already told you. Pa always went out to the highway for the mail. If she wrote, it never got to us."

Masters hesitated, not wanting to hurt this woman but seeing no way to avoid it. "She didn't write to tell you that she had a child?"

Abel jumped to his feet. "Ain't so!" he cried.

Mrs. Carter stood up. "Shush, Abel." She turned to Masters. "I found out about it last night." She rummaged in her pocketbook and produced an envelope. She handed it to Masters, at the same time glancing at Abel. "I didn't want to tell about this but the time has come I got to. Didn't want Abel to know. He ain't seen it yet, Sheriff. You read it out."

Masters took the envelope from her, glancing at the postmark as he did so. The letter was two weeks old. He took out the single sheet of paper it contained. Feeling like an intruder, he read aloud from the clear, round handwriting:

"Dear Ma," it began. *"It's been a long time since I wrote last. I waited and waited to hear from you but I guess you were too mad at me to write. The baby was born all right and I didn't have much trouble. It was a boy but I never did get to see him. They adopted him right out to some rich people, they told me. Why I am writing is because I have a good job now in Clay City and I am being good and I would like to come and visit you if you think Pa wouldn't make trouble. There is a bus that leaves on Sundays at nine and I could be there by eleven.*

"Well I am fine. I am staying at a hotel called the

*Oceanus House in case you want to write me and
say that it will be all right to come up there to see
you. I would like very much to see you, Ma, and
Abel. But don't say it's all right if Pa will make
trouble.*

*"Well I guess I will close this now because I have
to go to work and I hope you are fine, and Abel.
And I hope it will be all right for me to come.*

"Lovingly, Lucy."

Masters felt a cold, deep rage. "You never got the
other letter, did you." He made it a statement, not a
question.

Mrs. Carter shook her head. "I never got any letter.
I never would have got this one except that I went
through Joachim's papers. I never done that since we
were married."

Masters looked toward Abel. The youth had buried
his face in his big hands; his shoulders were shaking.
Mrs. Carter walked over to stand beside him. She
dropped one hand on his shoulder. "Mrs. Lafferty told
me about the man who killed hisself last night; says
people are saying he done it because he killed my
Lucy. That ain't so, Sheriff. Joachim killed my girl.
You find out where he was a week ago Monday. That
was after the letter came—you can tell from the date.
He got in the car and he went off and he didn't come
back till long past midnight. Same thing last Sunday,
the night she was killed. He was gone almost all night.
Ain't that so, Abel?"

The boy looked up. He seemed to brace himself,
squaring his shoulders and setting his jaw. "That's
right, Ma. I filled the tank on the car Saturday.
Monday it was almost empty."

Mrs. Carter continued: "I heard somewheres a wife
can't testify or bear witness against her husband.

Joachim always preaches an eye for an eye and a tooth for a tooth. I want him to die like he killed my girl." She fumbled again in her handbag and brought out a blue bandanna handkerchief. "This is Joachim's. I found it in the car the day you came out to see us with Sheriff Byrd. It's got blood on it."

Masters said quietly, "You're wrong about a wife testifying against a husband. You can't be made to if you don't want to, but if you do, I'll see that you get the chance. Did he make any trouble about you coming down to the funeral this morning?"

Abel answered, "He didn't know we were coming. He went off yesterday noontime to look at some feeder cattle over Milledgeville way. He generally takes a couple days 'fore he finds what he wants." He added frankly, "I was scared about leaving. We mind what Pa says, most times, but Ma wanted to come for Lucy's funeral. If I'd 'a knowed about that letter—or about the blood—I wouldn't have been scared. I'm strongen't than he is. I'd 'a half killed him and brought him to you myself."

Masters got up and strode to the telephone. "Get me Sheriff Sam Byrd in Simontown," he said.

Sam Byrd, when Masters had identified himself, sounded grim. "I'd have called you if you hadn't called first," he said. "The R.F.D. carrier took a letter from Clay City to Joachim Carter's mailbox two weeks ago. Remembers it because he only gets mail once a month or so for Carter."

Masters' voice was equally grim. "I know Sam," he said. "I've got the letter with me now. It may turn out to be a death warrant. I've got word that Carter has gone to Milledgeville—touring the country looking over feeder stock for fall. If I don't get him and he gets back to Simontown, pick him up. Hold him on a charge of suspicion of murder."

CHAPTER ELEVEN

There was relief in direct action after the frustration of negative leads and indefinite conclusions. Masters, moving swiftly, flung the massed resources of the highway patrol, the sheriffs' radio network and the local police into the search for Joachim Carter. He did this by telephone conversation with Jake Bowen at the courthouse, with Abel Carter furnishing the make of Carter's car, its license number and color. When he had finished with Bowen he made an effort to persuade Mrs. Carter and her son to stay with Martha Lafferty until such time as Joachim would be picked up. Mrs. Carter refused.

"I ain't scared of him no more. Not with Abel with me," she said stubbornly. "When you want to get me to testify against him, you can find me home. You just let Sheriff Sam Byrd know when you get him—or call Jim Dreyer. Tell them to let me know. I want to know just as soon as you arrest him."

Masters was impatient to get down to the courthouse but he delayed long enough to try to change Mrs. Carter's mind.

"If he killed your daughter," he said, "he'll know that you're dangerous to him. Sheriff Byrd will be watching for him. I doubt if he can get by to get to your place but there's a chance that he might. I still think you'd be safer here."

Abel Carter shook his head. "Ma and me will go home," he said. "Just you let us know when you get him. Just you let us know."

Masters made hasty arrangements for Martha Lafferty to drive the Carters to the bus depot and left the house.

He could sense the tension in the air when he strode into his office. The usually phlegmatic Jake Bowen had the telephone receiver jammed against his right ear and he was talking in terse monosyllables. Tom Danning had brought out a long-barreled target revolver and he was absently spinning the cylinder while he watched Bowen. Masters recognized the smell of a manhunt in the little room. Bowen, seeing Masters, edged from behind the desk, still talking into the mouthpiece.

"Yeah, yeah," he said. "Sure. Well, you let us know, hear?" He hung up. "That was Milledgeville," he explained. "Carter left there couple of hours ago. Bought twenty head of stock from a breeder. Said he was heading toward Marietta. That would put him on route forty-six and he'd pass east of here about ten miles."

Masters said, "Call the highway patrol so they can put it on their radio. You, Tom, put it on the sheriffs' network." While the two deputies carried out his brief orders Masters turned to Bob Dunn. "You still want to go back to Atlanta?" he asked.

Dunn shook his head. "I don't want to, Ed, but I'm committed. I called this morning and said I'd be in before night. I'm due to testify in a murder trial tomorrow and we've already had three postponements. I'll come on back down after the trial if you need me or you can send on anything you want lab work done on. It looks like a fairly clear-cut case here—the Carter affair, I mean. You've got testimony from the man's own wife that he killed the girl. I got that much from Jake's end of the conversation with you. What did he do—admit it to her?"

Masters shook his head. "No. But he was away from home the night she was killed. He used a lot of gasoline, according to the boy. And Mrs. Carter found this in the car yesterday after I went out there to talk to him." Masters handed Dunn the bloodstained bandanna handkerchief that Mrs. Carter had given him, "How long would it take for you to process this?"

Dunn rubbed his chin and said doubtfully, "Couple of hours. Can it wait until after the trial tomorrow? I'll phone you back."

Masters nodded. "Guess so. We haven't got Carter yet. Are you still convinced that George Cox was a suicide?"

Dunn said, almost testily, "I haven't changed my mind, Ed. If he didn't do it out of remorse for having killed the Carter girl, he still had plenty of reasons left. He'd been exposed as a liar and a thief and worse."

Masters smiled. "I wasn't trying to aggravate you, Bob. Fact is, Carter was away from home last night too. You'll call me, then?"

Dunn agreed and left the office.

Then began for Masters and his deputies a period of fretting. There were no further steps to be taken toward apprehending Joachim Carter. It was a time for patience but Masters ran short of it. He sent Jake Bowen out to dig for more evidence to make a case against Benny Zurich on his original charge of operating a public nuisance. Bowen protested the assignment, an unusual action for him. Masters understood. Knowing his men, he also knew that a manhunt was the high point of their duty. He had seen it before, most recently when a child had strayed into the nearby Crying Woman Swamp, a desolate two-hundred-square-mile wilderness of bitter water and Spanish moss, of gumbo mud and quaking hammocks of saw grass. The object of the manhunt had been merciful then. Even the schism between Chief Trowbridge's department and his own office had temporarily been bridged over while a thousand quietly determined men had worked around the clock to push a wedge deep into the swamp. Big Trucks, he remembered, had found the child. He still had a picture of the big policeman, his face raw with scratches and insect bites, wading out of the muck like some prehistoric monster, cradling the child—scared but alive—in his tremendous arms.

After Bowen left, Charlie Hess came in. The reporter was less exuberant, less aggressive than usual. He seemed tired and strained. "I've been over at Trowbridge's office," he said. "I telephoned in what you put out to the highway patrol. There was just time for a bulletin on the front page of the last edition. I promised to get something on the wire later. The wire services have been driving me crazy." He made the final comment in an odd, almost proud manner.

Tom Danning asked curiously, "Do they pay you extra on a thing like that, Charlie?"

Hess shook his head. "No," he said. "We get a retainer for protecting them. But it doesn't do any harm to get your name in front of the bigshot editors in Atlanta and Charleston. Have they picked up the old man yet?"

Masters said, "Not yet."

Hess remained only long enough to be brought up to date on Masters' activities. He stood up and said, "Guess I'd better get on back to the office and keep the AP and the UP happy. They're making a big thing of this case, Ed."

Masters, half amused, waved a hand as Hess went out. He glanced at the clock. It was lacking three minutes to five o'clock when the telephone rang for the twentieth time in the last hour. Tom Danning picked it up, listened for a moment and handed the instrument to Masters.

"You better take this, Ed," he said excitedly. "I think

they got him."

Masters reached out a big hand for the telephone identified himself. The caller was State Police Sergeant Schuster from the barracks half a dozen miles from Clay City. Masters recollected dealings with Schuster, who had, in the past, been critical about county law enforcement. This time his expression was tinged with apologetic embarrassment.

"Look, Sheriff," he said. "This Carter guy. One of my troopers picked him up half an hour ago over on highway forty-six."

Masters interrupted him. "Where is he bringing him?"

The sergeant answered bitterly, "That's the hell of it. He got away. The trooper is here now, Sheriff. You want to come on out to the barracks or do you want me to have him get on the phone?"

Masters said, "I'll come on out there," and hung up.

He drove the six miles to the barracks in ten minutes, punishing the car in an unaccustomed fury. The sergeant came to meet him in the entry, saying, "Well, hell, Sheriff, I'm sorry about this. Don't be too hard on the kid. He got outsmarted."

The sergeant led the way to his own office. The trooper who had arrested Joachim Carter—he was hardly more than a boy—was seated on a hard wooden chair, nervously twisting his uniform cap between his hands. When he saw his sergeant entering with Masters on his heels he stood up, dropped the cap and picked it up again. The sergeant said, "This is trooper Hunt, Sheriff Masters. Bob Hunt." He added, speaking to the trooper, "Go ahead. Tell him about it."

Masters felt himself fighting to hold in his anger. Now that Joachim Carter was warned that he was wanted, he would be that much harder to catch. At the same time the sheriff found it hard to punish the trooper any more than he was punishing himself. In obvious embarrassment, Hunt began his explanation. "I got the call on the radio," he said. "I was patrolling route forty-six going north when I saw this car up ahead of me. Looked like an old Buick. The color was right, dark blue. I speeded up and came up behind it to look at the license plate. It checked, so I pulled ahead and crowded him to the side of the road. He didn't try to speed up or anything—just pulled in as soon as he saw the spotlight on the patrol car."

The sergeant said accusingly, "You didn't call in right then like you should have. What were you doing— trying to play hero?"

Hunt reddened and shook his head. "It wasn't that way," he said. "Honest to God, I was just too busy making the pinch to think about it."

Masters said, "Get on with it, Hunt."

"I pulled in hard in front of him so he couldn't pull ahead while I got out of my car." Hunt shook his head. "He was an old gaffer but your bulletin said he was wanted on suspicion of murder so I didn't take any chances. I had my service pistol drawn when I jumped out of the car and I yelled at him to get out from behind the wheel and to bend over the fender with his hands on the hood of the car."

Hunt made the last statement almost by rote and with a faint air of defiance, looking directly at Schuster as he spoke. The sergeant grunted. "All right," he said, "so you read the manual. Tell us what you said then. Make it word for word."

Hunt lost any remaining defiance. "I said, 'Is your name Joachim Carter?' The old guy had done just what I ordered him to so far. I figured I'd scared hell out of him what with the gun and the way I yelled at him. He said over his shoulder, 'My name is Joachim Carter and what the devil do you mean by stopping me?'"

Hunt lowered his voice slightly. "And I said, 'You're talking pretty big for a man who murdered his own daughter.'"

The sergeant drew in his breath sharply but said nothing. Masters, who had been feeling a growing sympathy for the trooper, changed his mind. A rash, thoughtless act he could understand and forgive. The trooper, in tipping his hand for the sake of whatever satisfaction it gave him to bulldoze Carter, had been more stupid than rash. He said wearily, "What did you do then?"

"Well, I started toward him to get his billfold and papers and to see if he had a gun." He blurted the rest of it. "He was an old man; you know that. I didn't expect anything and I got too close. He kicked out at me like a damn mule. Caught me right in the crotch."

Schuster said disgustedly, "My God, what a bonehead you turned out to be."

"I couldn't get my wind. It was like knives were sticking in me, in my chest and in my gut. I dropped my gun and keeled over and he jumped me and grabbed the gun off the ground. He fired twice and I thought he was shooting at me and then I saw he'd shot holes in the two rear tires of the patrol car. Before I could get up he jumped into his own car and backed up and turned back south."

Masters asked, "Did he say anything at all while this was going on?"

Hunt nodded. "He was mumbling something, more like he was talking to himself than to me. I couldn't make out any words."

"Did he take the gun with him?"

"Yeah. And he turned off the road while he was still in sight. I got over to the car and called in what had happened and asked the sergeant to send a car out for me."

Schuster said, "Tell him what I told you, Hunt. Go on—tell him."

Hunt protested weakly, "Aw, hell, sarge—"

The sergeant said coldly, "Don't 'sarge' me, you jackass. And tell him what I told you."

Hunt mumbled, "You said to walk in if I couldn't bum a ride."

The sergeant said, "That's enough. Now get the hell out of my office." When Hunt had shambled from the room he turned to Masters. "I'm sorry it happened, Sheriff. I'm doing what I can to make up for it. I've got cars out looking and I've asked the National Guard for a helicopter. You know that country, I guess?"

Masters lit his pipe. "Hunt didn't say which way he turned off. If it was east, we'll need dogs too."

The sergeant shrugged. "I already sent for the hounds. It was east. If we don't get him in an hour he'll be in Crying Woman and we'll have to seine him out."

Masters said, "I don't think you'll get him. There are a thousand roads in through the thickets that they made when they logged off the pine woods thirty years ago. Your patrol cars won't be able to use them but he can. That's one reason the back-country people use old cars. They're not low slung and they don't hang up in the ruts." He stood up. "Assuming he gets into Crying Woman—and that's what I'm going to do— you don't have enough men to handle it. It's my county and my case and I'll need a posse of men that know their way around in the swamps. We'll work in from both sides and we'll use your people to keep in communication with the patrol car radios—if you're agreeable."

"What you mean is you don't want the troopers getting lost in the swamps and doing any more harm than Hunt has already done."

Masters smiled. "I didn't say it."

"You could have and I wouldn't blame you."

Masters drove back to the courthouse at a more reasonable speed. There was no great need for haste now. Either the troopers of the highway patrol would get Joachim Carter before he got into Crying Woman or they wouldn't. If they didn't, a lot of preliminary work would have to be done before men could be sent into the swamp.

Toward dusk the streets of Clay City began to clot with men. Farmers, in from the country and carrying shotguns. City men, some of them with hunting rifles A sprinkling from the pool rooms and bars; these the loudest talkers. All of them drifted toward the courthouse, where Ed Masters maintained a sort of command post. They stayed outside the building, gathering in small groups on the patch of green lawn that surrounded the statue of a local general who fought and died in the Civil War.

Masters watched from the window of his office. Of these men, the bulk would go out bravely enough to hunt Joachim Carter down, forgetting the maddening insects, the dangerous morasses, the sticky heat and the slashing saw grass that grew head high in places and could cut a man's face to ribbons in the darkness. Within a couple of hours, fifty per cent of the men would give it up as a bad job and go home. Another ten per cent would stop to take on a few drinks of corn whisky. Somebody always had a jug on these occasions. The jug would pass around until it was empty and then there would be an exodus in search of more. The city sports would be next to fall out of the ranks. Not because they wanted to, particularly, but because they would become physically exhausted and would actually hamper the others. Masters, knowing his men, knowing Crying Woman, could count on a hard core of perhaps twenty men, swamp-wise men, to do the actual searching for Joachim Carter. Of these he planned to deputize half a dozen; these would lead the various parties cutting into the swamp from four sides.

Masters would have preferred to wait for daylight before getting the manhunt under way. The chances of finding Carter at night were slim and he was armed and dangerous, but the word had gone out, the men were gathered and they were less apt to kill themselves or lose themselves in the swamp if the search was organized.

Sergeant Schuster called in at eight by previous arrangement. The patrolmen who had gone into the pine barrens surrounding the swamp had found no trace of Joachim Carter or his car. The National Guard helicopter had had less than an hour of daylight by the time the pilot had it airborne and he had returned to his base, having seen no trace of the fugitive. Schuster had one more or less encouraging piece of information. "We've got the bloodhounds here," he said. "They got here about fifteen minutes ago from Valdosta barracks."

Masters said, "I'll meet you at your barracks as soon as I get my people organized. Say half an hour. Don't start with the dogs until I get there."

He turned from the phone. "Jake," he said, "get Morgan, Bates and Ewart in here. Get Morris, Stifler and Combs." While Jake was gone the sheriff fumbled in the drawer of his desk for the badges he would issue to the six swamp veterans he intended to deputize.

They filed quickly and silently into the room—lean men, all of them. They knew the routine; they wasted no time in greetings other than a casual, "'Lo, Ed."

Masters held up his right hand and they followed suit, repeating after him the oath that made them deputies. They treated the formality of swearing in with a sort of casual contempt. Masters brought them up to date as quickly as he could on the Carter matter, emphasizing that Joachim was probably more than a little insane and consequently the more dangerous. Stifler, a pine woods cracker, shifted his shotgun from his right hand to his left. "Killed his own daughter, Ed?" he repeated.

Masters nodded. "Looks like it. So you be careful. You boys know what to do. You've done it before. Split up into four parties. Settle among yourselves which side of the swamp each man will take. Divide up the men outside that want to go along." He grinned. "Each man is supposed to carry his own share of tenderfeet. Split up the swamp men even. Two of you stay out with Tom Danning and set up a camp, east side of the swamp."

Stifler shuffled his feet. "Those men outside. You want us to tell them what you told us about Carter? Some of them boys might not want to bring him in alive was they to know what he done."

Masters said, "You better tell them the straight of it. They'll get wind of it anyway. That's all, boys. I'm going out to see about the hounds." He was mildly surprised that Charlie Hess didn't turn up to make a nuisance of himself. Probably covering himself with glory for the wire services, he decided.

Schuster was waiting impatiently when Masters drove up for the second time in a matter of hours. He shouted, "Follow me in your car," and got behind the wheel of a highway patrol cruiser, leaving a cloud of red clay dust for the sheriff to chase.

There was another patrol car pulled off the road at the point where Schuster slammed his own brakes on. A young, slim man in patrol uniform stood beside the car holding two bloodhounds on leash. They were big for hounds, Masters noted, with infinitely sad eyes set in ridiculously corrugated foreheads, and heavy chops that hung like the wattles of a turkey. The young trooper asked, "You ready, sergeant?"

Schuster said, "Yeah. We've wasted enough time. Sheriff, this is trooper Stewart. He trained the hounds. Stewart, this is Sheriff Ed Masters. This is his party."

Masters nodded at Stewart. "This where Carter got out of the car?" he asked.

Schuster grunted. "Yeah. I had that boneheaded Hunt take me out here. There's a few tracks but they don't show much. You can see the spot where Hunt got knocked on his ass, though. And you can make out a few of Carter's tracks."

"I hope you don't expect too much, Sheriff," Stewart said. "These are good dogs. I don't know of none better, but people expect miracles sometimes. From what I hear, this Carter got back in his own car and drove off from here and turned in down in the pine woods between here and the swamp. If those pine barrens are anything like the ones down Valdosta way there must be dozens of log roads he could have taken. The hounds can't track a car. Sometimes, if the wind is just right and there's a little dew, they can follow a car by the scent of the man inside it but it's too dry this time of year."

Masters nodded. "I've worked with bloodhounds before," he said. He turned to fumble in the back seat of his own car, emerging with a worn pair of heavy work shoes. "These ought to be enough to give them the scent. They're Carter's." When Schuster looked surprised, Masters explained: "When it began to look as if we might have to go into the swamp after him with dogs I telephoned the sheriff of Carter's county.

Had him pick these up and send them down on the Greyhound bus. They got here half an hour ago."

Stewart said enthusiastically, "Couldn't ask for anything better. If we find where he left his car and went on foot, I swear these babies will find him."

Masters said, "That's a pretty big if with daylight gone. I've got men coming into the swamp from four directions, though. If he didn't hide it damn well, they'll find it—and get in touch with you by radio to the patrol car. Meantime, we can take the dogs east on the chance they might pick up a wind-borne scent this side of the swamp."

There was a quarter-moon hanging low in the west when Masters, Schuster, Stewart and the dogs came to the border of Crying Woman. Jake Bowen was manning the relay station, passing information along to the hunters. The dogs were restive, uneasy. They knew they weren't doing what they were bred and trained to do, Masters supposed. On the off chance that they had passed Carter's car in the darkness without seeing it, the men eased into the swamp itself on the trail of Stifler and his group of perhaps fifteen men who had gone in ahead of them. Stifler and his party were only a hundred yards or so ahead but they had already disappeared except for the occasional wink of a light that found an open path in the tangled mass of bramble and saw grass. Only an infrequent snatch of sound drifted back to them. It was as if the swamp resented their passage, closing in behind the men as swiftly as they passed. Masters, picking his way carefully, nevertheless stumbled thigh deep into one of the thousands of channels of brown water that threaded the swamp like a network of veins before he was five minutes in. Thereafter he stopped trying to keep dry and concentrated on protecting his face from the whipping, slashing saw grass.

The dogs, after an hour of the swamp, were in a pitiable state. Stewart said softly, "It'll take me a half a day to get the ticks off 'em, Sheriff. They can't even get a ground scent here."

Masters paused. "Guess you're right," he said. "Take 'em on out and get 'em rested up. We'll find the car with daylight and they can track him from there."

Schuster had been making heavy weather of it and Masters had noted this. Knowing that the sergeant would cut out his tongue before he would admit that it was harder for him than for the sheriff, Masters added, "We might just as well all get out of this. If the men that are in here already don't find him, there isn't much chance that we will without the dogs."

On solid ground again, Masters made brief arrangements for a cordon of highway patrolmen to keep an all-night surveillance of the roads leading out of the immediate area of the swamp and called in to Jake Bowen with instructions to recall the searchers as rapidly as they got in touch with the search headquarters. One group of men had already come out of the swamp and made a fire to brew coffee. Masters joined them for a cup, parrying the questions they asked him, enjoying the brief companionship but reserving his thoughts. It came to him that he might have been stampeded into thinking Carter had gone into Crying Woman—or that Hunt had been stampeded, deliberately misled by Carter. Then again, Carter was swamp-wise. He lived beside the Oconee, which had its own swamps. On the run, hiding from the law, he would know the advantage his knowledge gave him, and he would most likely seek the sanctuary of Crying Woman.

It came to him as he drove toward home that he had been nursing a small doubt about the certainty of Carter's guilt. The man's absences from home could be explained, possibly. So could the blood on the bandanna handkerchief that his wife had handed to the sheriff. Men who work with farm tools, with livestock and barbed wire, habitually carry cut scars. But by running, Carter had indicted himself. Why, barring guilty knowledge of the crime that Hunt had confronted him with, would he have run?

Masters showered the swamp muck from his body in Martha Lafferty's gleaming bathroom and shuffled in bathrobe and slippers to the kitchen for a glass of milk. While he was drinking it another question offered itself for consideration: Why, in God's name, had Joachim Carter stripped the dress—the yellow dress—from the dead body of his daughter? Masters turned the question over, examined it and could find no answer. He shrugged it off and went back to his room for what sleep he could get against the morning. It was 10:50 p.m. and he planned to get back to Crying Woman at first light. Some of the thrill seekers would have dropped out of the posse by that time but his hard core, he was certain, would be early for the hunt. He needed his sleep, but as he lay down and thought of Carter and felt the tension moving through him, he knew there would be little of it for this night.

CHAPTER TWELVE

She swung down from the cab of a big red diesel truck where the highway diverged to bypass Clay City: a girl in her early twenties, small enough so that the distance from the running board of the big trailer hitch to the ground was too big for her to step. Instead she jumped, clutching her overnight case in one hand while she waved to the driver with the other.

A nice guy, she thought. All the dusty miles down

from Carolina he had laughed and kidded with her. Bought her hamburgers and coffee in Jonesboro and, when it was dark and she sort of half looked for it, he hadn't tried to maul her. Until the fork in the road here, and then it had been: "This is where I head west, Red. I'll put up just this side of the Florida line after I drop the hitch. There's a nice motel if you're interested."

She hadn't been and she told him so and that had been that. No hard feelings. No nastiness like making a grab for her breasts when being a nice guy didn't buy him anything. Come to think of it, she never had hitched a ride with a truck driver yet but what he turned out to be a good guy. She wouldn't have minded going on with him except that there were plenty of jobs in the mills in Clay City. Everybody knew that. Spindle doffers and perchers, draw-in hands and slasher tenders. Florida was something, and she wasn't going to arrive there broke. She would stop in Clay City and get a job in the mills for a few weeks. Save a hundred dollars to go with what she already had and then—Miami, here's Red!

There weren't many cars—not as many as she had hoped there would be. Couldn't be much more than ten-thirty but that was a bad hour for hitchhiking in a way, because most of the cars now would be full of young guys out juking. Liquored up and inclined to be nasty. After five minutes in the darkness she began to hope for any kind of car, jukers or not, and she nearly regretted that she had not gone on in the big trailer.

Then came a glow behind her, rapidly increasing in intensity and dividing to become two headlights. She moved out nearer the road and smiled hopefully but with a faint reserve that said, "I don't really care if you pick me up or not, mister." Actually, of course, she did care. What with the weird noises from the woods to her left and right and the lonely blackness of the night, she was close to panic. The car came on with a growling mutter and she edged still nearer to the center of the road. In the lights of the car she was quite small, quite thin, with little breasts that she thrust out now, squaring her shoulders to do so and turning slightly so that the driver could see that she had nice legs. She wanted a ride that much. When the driver smashed at the brakes so that the tires howled she prepared still another smile, one of gratitude and good fellowship this time. But he wasn't stopping; he was merely veering out to be sure he missed her. She watched him go, near to tears in her fright and disappointment, indifferent to the wind of the car's passing that lifted her skirt halfway up her thighs.

Couldn't make any money here. She gripped the overnight case more firmly and began to walk. Six miles away was Clay City but there would be a car before that. She promised herself that there would be another car.

One came, from Clay City, not toward it, and she hugged the side of the road, wasting no smile, or anything else, on a car that was headed away from Florida. Minutes later another car, from the right direction this time, and again she made the most of face and figure, even pulling her skirt up a little above her knee with the hand that held the case, as if it were by accident.

It was a heavy car and again the driver had to smash at the brakes and even so he didn't get the car stopped until he was thirty feet beyond her. She ran toward it so as not to keep him waiting, wondering—but not really caring—if he was alone, or if he was young or old. Inside the car she still couldn't tell. The dashboard light was dim and he kept his face straight ahead.

She said, when she had her breath, "Gee, I'm glad you stopped, mister. I was scared out there." She made herself sound as naïve as she could on the theory that if you acted like a kid, guys sometimes were ashamed to make passes. Sometimes.

He said nothing, keeping his head stiffly turned toward the road. One of those, she decided. The kind that tried to make you feel like dirt because they were behind the wheel of a car and you were hitchhiking. Big shots. Big shots, little shots, any of them wanted whatever they could get and she squeezed toward the door so that he couldn't—if he wanted to—put his hand on her legs, just by mistake, of course. She lit a cigarette, offering him one from her own pack first. He shook his head slightly, not saying anything; and when she lit up she tried to make out his face in the flare of the match. At that moment he slowed the car violently and made a skidding turn onto a side road. The car hadn't slowed enough for the turn and the tires howled again.

She made her voice as hard and indignant as she could. "All right, mister," she said. "This isn't the road to town. Let me out and go get yourself some other company."

He stopped the car suddenly so that she rocked forward and her head hit the dashboard. It was painful enough to bring the tears to her eyes but she kept her voice steady. Here came the pass. Now he would try to fondle her, to get his hand under her dress. "You dirty bastard," she said, and reached out to fend off his reaching hands, more angry than scared now.

When she felt metal slicing into her palm she was scared again, but it was too late. She fought to push the hands away, not wasting her breath in futile screaming, but she was quite small and not very strong and it was easy for him to brush the hands aside and find her small breasts with the knife.

When it was over he moved quickly, sliding out his own side and coming around to her door. He had a raincoat in his hands and he slipped it around her limp body and lifted her out before any blood could soak through her clothing onto the upholstery of the car. Within minutes he was back in the car again.

He drove in deep thought for several minutes, aware of the harsh rasp of his own breathing over the heavy drone of the motor. A mile after he had turned onto the highway, he thought of something and he stopped briefly while he hurled the knife he had used into the underbrush beside the road. Not that it was necessary but a man had to be careful. When he started the car again he felt an overwhelming impulse to laugh. This he diagnosed as pure nervous reaction, compounded with relief. He checked himself as he remembered that the relief was premature. What if Masters had caught Carter? What if Carter was right now, right this minute, sitting in a cell, waiting to point a finger at him and say heavily, "I know that man." He could picture Masters slowly turning toward him, the iron look that would come over the face of the sheriff and his deputies.

Two hours earlier he had heard the news of Carter's arrest and escape and he had driven out here looking for him with no real hope of success. But he had been unable to sit and wait for the word to come from Crying Woman that they had him. He had wondered idly why Carter was running. Maybe, knowing how much she hated him, Carter had guessed that his wife would accuse him of killing his daughter. God, but that had been a break, an unbelievable break. And, in a way, Carter had it coming.

Then he had seen the girl on the highway and made his decision. It was a gamble that her body would be found before they got Carter, but actually he was risking very little because if they took Carter—alive— it was all over for him anyway. If they did find the body first, then they would blame Carter and the hunt for him would intensify. A fugitive with the murder of his daughter and an innocent hitchhiker on his hands could be shot down like a wild pig, and no one would question the killing. Time was what he needed now. It was going to be a long night of waiting. When he put his car away he locked Red's suitcase in the trunk. It might be useful.

Ed Masters was already awake when his telephone rang. He picked it up and identified himself. Sergeant Schuster was on the other end of the wire. His voice was taut. "We've found a girl's body, Masters," he said. "That son of a bitch must have got by us last night."

Masters, who had given the order recalling the manhunters for the night, said, "If he did, it's my responsibility. You sure it was Carter?"

"Pretty damn sure," Schuster said, "You'll see what I mean when you get here."

Masters asked for quick directions and broke the connection abruptly. He dressed swiftly, strapping on a shell belt and a rarely carried pistol. He was convinced now that Carter, a religious fanatic, was insane.

Schuster had promised to be waiting in front of the combination filling station and general store from which he had called. Masters, driving with the county car all out, saw Schuster's car and a moment later Schuster himself as he raced from the door of the building. The sergeant flung the door open and slid into the front seat before the car had completely stopped. "That side road, hundred yards down there," he said.

There was a second highway patrol car parked with its left wheels in the ditch a short distance up the side road onto which Masters turned. The trooper who manned the car was holding back a knot of half a dozen men who were talking among themselves in the preoccupied manner of men come face to face with tragedy. When he saw Schuster and Masters the trooper came forward. "She's in there," he said to Masters. "Old fella, says his name is Chappie, found her when he left his shack this morning to hunt mushrooms."

Masters searched the gathering of men with a swift glance. An old colored man, a little aloof from the others, he identified at once as Chappie Williams, handy man to three generations of Clay City householders. Masters beckoned to him.

"How long ago did you find her, Chappie?" he asked.

Chappie was close to eighty, Masters knew, and yet his face was almost unlined. "'Bout an hour ago, She'ff Masters," he said in a deep bass. "Come out to find mushrooms while the dew was still fresh and I found her layin' like she is in there. I run down to the filling station as soon as ever I see'd her and banged on the door till Mister Parker let me in. I told the operator to give me the police and she connected me with these gentlemen from the barracks."

Masters glanced about him. The roadside was lined on both sides with thickets of huckleberry and sumac. The unpainted shanty that he knew to be the home of old Chappie was the only structure for half a mile in either direction.

"Did you hear or see anything last night?" he asked.

"Come sundown, this old man goes to bed, She'ff. I didn't hear nothin' or see nothin' till I come out here and found her like I told you."

"Didn't see any cars stop? See any headlights?"

Chappie shook his head. "Only cars come out here off the highway is young folks. Sometimes they stop and they's carryin' on so I minds my own business."

Masters nodded. "Thanks, Chappie," he said. He looked around for Schuster and found him on hands and knees in the dust, searching the roadside.

"When did it rain last, Masters?" he asked, standing erect.

"Couple of days. You won't find any tracks," Masters answered. "The ground is baked like cement. You could drive a Sherman tank along the road without leaving sign." He asked a question of his own. "Did you call the coroner after you notified me?"

"Yeah. He should be along any time now. You want to go on in the brush while we wait for him to show up?"

"Might as well." The two men walked carefully into the huckleberry thicket, both of them searching the ground with alert eyes.

The body, face down, seemed pathetically, almost unreasonably small and crumpled. Masters approached it carefully, wishing that Bob Dunn were here with his equipment. "Stabbed," he said. "More than once; there's a lot of blood."

Schuster grunted. "More than once. More than a dozen times. I lifted her up by the shoulders enough to see. I wanted to get a look at her face. She wasn't much more than a kid."

"Recognize her?" Masters asked.

"Nah."

Both men, after a few moments and by a mutual, unspoken agreement, withdrew from the body, Masters to light his pipe, Schuster a cigarette. The sheriff glanced at his watch; it was close to seven-thirty and already the sun's heat was beginning to be oppressive. The sergeant's forehead was peppered with tiny beads of sweat. He wiped them away with his sleeved forearm and said, "I can't blame the boys too much, Masters. There are so many of those old log roads that it would be next to impossible to put an airtight block on them. Where do you figure he went from here?"

Masters had been thinking about that same problem. He said slowly, "He's crazy. Crazy as a tick. You ever notice that the crazy ones sometimes act in the simplest and most direct manner?"

Schuster said doubtfully, "Yeah. I guess so."

"When Hunt stopped him yesterday and told him he was wanted for murder he ran for the swamp, knowing he had a chance to get away in there. Turned out he got away. We didn't catch him."

Schuster nodded. "Then he'll have gone back to Crying Woman."

Masters tapped his pipe against the sole of his shoe. "I'd say so. Once you get out of the barrens and away from the swamp, there aren't many roads. I think your people would have picked him up by this time if he'd gone to the highway. I think he knows it too."

There was a grumble of motors from the highway. Masters stretched, wishing for a cup of coffee. "That will be the coroner. Probably one of my deputies too."

Doc Adams, his face gaunt and strained, came plowing through the brush followed by Jake Bowen and Charlie Hess. Masters counted the days back to Monday morning when these men had made an almost identical entrance to the glade off the Kingsbridge Pike and was startled to find that there were only two intervening mornings. In his present mood of self-accusation for having called off the hunt for Joachim Carter it seemed that a month had gone by since they had found the body of Lucy Carter lying in the loblollies. He knew it would have been stupid to keep the men in the swamps hunting for Carter in the darkness. Stupid and dangerous. But the mood stayed with him.

Doc Adams made no protest at being called from his bed, in itself an indication of the old man's weariness. He went directly to the body and bent down to turn it over. Masters turned away and beckoned to Bowen, who came up and muttered in a low voice, "Carter?"

Masters said, "Looks like it. Get on back to town, Jake. Pass the word about what's happened here. I'll want enough men to go into Crying Woman and look under every bush, if necessary. Call the radio station. They'll help. And get hold of Tom Danning. Tell him to get on the phone and check every report he can get his hands on of missing women. Take a look for yourself; make a few notes on what she's wearing and her general description. Doc will give you a guess on her age."

Jake Bowen nodded and walked away. Masters turned to Charlie Hess. The reporter seemed to have lost assurance and with it a good share of his bandbox appearance. His eyes were tired and he needed a shave. The sheriff said somberly, "You'll have company from the Atlanta papers when they get word of this, I suppose."

Hess said absently, "I guess so. They were keeping the teletype busy when I left the office last night. That was after the old man got away from the trooper. They may be big-city papers but they're still Southerners underneath it. A manhunt is the top story of them all."

Masters said, "I guess." Hess, he thought, probably resented the fact that the real professionals from the bigger papers would be coming now to take over what he considered to be his own story.

The reporter lit a cigarette and puffed nervously at

it before he asked, "The girl over there. Did you find a bag yet?"

Masters shook his head. "Not unless it's underneath her and I doubt that it is. Sergeant Schuster lifted her up part way. He probably would have seen it." He lifted his voice to call to Doc Adams, "Any sign of a pocketbook, Doc?"

When the coroner silently shook his head Masters said, "There's your answer. You didn't see her yet, Charlie. When Doc is through look at her and see if you know her."

Hess said, "Sure, Ed. What do you plan to do now? They'll be raising hell back in town."

"I can imagine," Masters answered dryly. "I can't do much that I haven't already done, Charlie. I'm going to wait and see what Doc Adams has to say. Then I'm going back to the office and see if Tom or Jake have a line on a missing girl. Right now I don't know if this girl was local or not. I don't even know that much." Masters glanced toward the body of the dead girl and as quickly looked away again. "Then," he continued, "I'm going into Crying Woman with every man I can get to come with me and I'm not coming out until I've got Carter."

Hess threw his cigarette to the ground and pawed at it with the toe of his shoe. "You seem pretty sure he's in there, Ed."

Masters said, "I'm pretty sure. We'll find his car first. In the daylight that shouldn't be too hard. Then we'll use the bloodhounds."

"I'm coming, Ed," Hess said. "Somebody from the city desk can handle the rest of the story. It will make a good first-person account—that is, if it's all right with you?"

"I told you I wanted every man I could get," Masters said. "You can ride out with me from my office if you

want. Meantime, take a look at the girl. Sing out if
you know her. If you don't, get as accurate a description
as you can in your story. Sergeant Schuster is going
to have his identification officer get pictures; I've got
Jake busy. I'll see that copies get sent to your paper as
soon as possible."

Doc Adams straightened from the body of the girl
and stood up slowly and painfully. Masters walked
toward him and looked down at the still face while
Jake Bowen and Charlie Hess came up to stand beside
him. After a moment Hess said, "I don't know her,
Ed."

Jake Bowen, at Masters' inquiring glance, shook his
head. "I don't either. You want me to do anything else
before I get on back to town, Ed?"

Masters said, "No," and Bowen left with Hess on his
heels. Masters turned to Doc Adams, who was busy
with his old-fashioned black bag. "When we get back
to town," he said softly, "I'm going to buy you a cup of
coffee. Right now I've got to get some answers from
you."

The coroner set the bag down. "I'm an old man, Ed,
and I'm downright testy sometimes. And I need my
coffee and my sleep. They can wait, this time, because
you better catch this man before he puts me in my
grave. Well. First: The cause of death, just like the
other one. Multiple stab wounds and loss of blood. It
took probably three or four minutes for her to die.
Second: Just like the other one again—a small knife.
The wounds are stab wounds, not cuts, and they aren't
very deep. All but three of the wounds are in the breast
and there was enough tissue so that the weapon didn't
actually reach the heart. There are three additional
wounds in the abdomen. Probably punctured the large
intestine. She's been dead since shortly before
midnight."

Masters asked quickly, "Can you tell if the three wounds were made before or after the other wounds?"

Doc Adams shook his head. "I can't. Nobody else can either. I don't see how that matters. The girl was in her early twenties; this side of twenty-five for sure. There is no sign of a sexual attack."

"That's the basic difference between this and the other one," Masters said. "Her dress appears to be intact."

Doc Adams nodded. "Might not mean anything. You can't really know unless you know why he took the dress from the other girl. The underclothing—what there is of it—seems to be intact also. I'll do an autopsy as soon as you can get her back to the morgue for me, but I think you can rely on what I've already told you."

Masters made hasty arrangements for a coroner's jury and arranged with Sergeant Schuster for a police guard to be posted at the scene of the murder before he drove back to the courthouse.

There was a difference in the very air of the city as Masters drove through the downtown section. As had been the case yesterday there were knots of men clotting the corners, talking in small groups. Many of them were armed. There was a different aspect, an indefinable shading in purpose that was not merely the result of a difference in composition in the crowd today. The men who had appeared yesterday were in the crowd. To it now were added other groups. Small businessmen, store clerks, doctors and barbers, their shops left closed.

Masters could almost have predicted the size and mood of the groups from past experience. Yesterday the manhunt had been bent on vengeance, the exaction of justice, and for that reason it had taken on some of the aspects of a carnival. Justice and vengeance were no longer the motivations of this manhunt. The women who had yesterday scolded their men, "Al (or Ray, or Joe), if you think you're going out chasing into that swamp half the night for that lunatic you've got another think coming. Let the sheriff get him. He's paid to do it," would now be silent in the face of yet another killing. The men would, most of them, not even have consulted their women. They would have quietly listened to the news broadcasts and as quietly gone to the closets or the attics for whatever weapon they happened to own. The women would have understood that this was, after all, a man's world and that men must band together for the defense of their homes and their women and few of them would have done other than lock the doors and prepare to wait until Joachim Carter was caught. This mob, then, was quieter than yesterday's. There would be less difficulty in controlling them, Masters knew. Until the moment that Carter was sighted—and then there might be some bad minutes.

Tom Danning was in the office with Jake Bowen. When he saw the sheriff, the deputy shook his head before he spoke. "Not a thing, Ed," he said. "We got the radio station to ask that anyone knowing of a missing girl call us here. The only report I got yet was from a woman who claims that a neighbor of hers has been missing for two days and that the husband says she went to Charlotte to visit a sick sister. She doesn't believe it, she claims. Says she thinks the husband did away with her. Only thing is, she weighs right on two hundred pounds and is in her fifties. The missing one, I mean."

"Stay with it. You'll get lots of calls when the cranks have had a chance to think it over. What about the regular reports?" Masters asked.

Danning said, "I've gone through all the missing

person reports and requests for information for the last six months. Nothing that comes close to matching the description Jake gave me. Did you look to see if there were any labels in her clothes, Ed?"

Masters said, "Doc Adams did. It was just light summer stuff. No labels. She may still have been a local girl. Could belong to a family that hasn't heard the broadcasts. Or she might not have a family to report her. Tell you what, Jake. Get on down to the Oceanus House. There's a clerk there by the name of Shaw. Little red-eyed fellow. Rout him out and describe the girl to him. See if he remembers anyone like her being registered in the last few months. If he even thinks he does, get him on out to where the girl is."

Bowen asked, "How about the Parks woman? Wouldn't she be apt to remember if the girl was one of the local crowd?"

Masters shook his head. "She's done enough already."

Tom Danning turned to Masters. "If she was a local girl of the type that stays out all night without anyone worrying, Ed, she might have hung out at Benny Zurich's place."

Masters frowned. "You mean I should have Benny picked up and brought in to see if he can identify her? Tom, that would amount to persecution. I could be accused of using the power of this office to satisfy personal prejudice. And now that I think about it, it's not a bad idea." He turned to Bowen and his voice hardened. "So we'll do it. Pick him up and hold him as a material witness."

Bowen grinned. "He ain't going to like it, Ed. He may even resist arrest."

Masters said quietly, "Your problem, Jake." It came to him as he spoke that it was a small thing, a mean thing, to be doing and that the action was probably born out of his own frustration and sense of failure over the fact that Joachim Carter had escaped to kill another time. Still, if Benny Zurich had not made Lucy Carter's own particular hell for her, he had taken advantage of it. As Cox had, and Cox was dead. As Joachim Carter had, and he was a fugitive.

He gave brief instructions to Tom Danning, who was to hold down the office, wished that there were time for a cup of coffee and decided that there wasn't and stepped out into the sunlight that by this time would have stripped some of the mystery from Crying Woman.

CHAPTER THIRTEEN

There were more than a hundred men in the group that had assembled in front of the courthouse by the time Masters emerged. These represented only part of the manhunt. The rest had gone out with Morgan and Stifler and the other swamp veterans. These had waited hoping that Masters would have some fresh information, some definite lead that would bring them the quicker to Joachim Carter. The men moved quietly and purposefully, not toward Masters but toward the cars which they had parked on the four sides of the square.

Masters, looking about, saw Charlie Hess standing beside the county car with his fiancée, Sally Martin. Masters touched the brim of his Stetson. "Hello, Sally," he said, and grinned at Charlie Hess. "She tell you you can't go with me into the swamps, Charlie, or is she waiting till after the wedding to start being the boss?"

The girl smiled. "I've already started, Sheriff, but I won't stop him from going with you. Charlie was supposed to drop me at the bank." The smile faded.

"That awful old man! Did you find out who the girl was yet, Sheriff?"

Masters moved around her to get into the driver's seat. "Not yet, Sally."

Charlie Hess was dressed in khaki shirt and trousers and a pair of leather moccasins. As Masters got into the car Hess reached into his hip pocket and spoke to the girl. "I've got my billfold with me with quite a bit of money and some important papers, Sally. I don't want to lose it crawling around in the muck and brush with Sheriff Masters. Put it in your pocketbook like a good girl until I get back, will you?"

She took it from him. Masters said a little impatiently, "Get in, Charlie, if you're coming with me."

Hess said, "No thanks, Ed. I'll take my own car. I've got my boots and my shotgun in it. Besides, I might want to come on back before you're ready."

Masters set out at the head of a long cavalcade to make the run to the point where Joachim Carter had yesterday broken away from trooper Hunt. Schuster had already agreed to meet him at that place with Stewart, the handler of the bloodhounds. Upon arrival he parked the car and got out to look at the long line of automobiles that had come after him. The country men parked in the road. The city men, some of them, tried to pull off out of habit and good driving discipline. More than a few of them, Masters knew, would bog down in spring holes and there would be a lot of geeing and hawing before they were put back on the road.

Schuster, red faced and irascible, came forward to meet him.

"Nothing yet," he said. "Not a damn thing. You want to start in with the dogs?"

Masters glanced at Stewart. The young trooper shook his head. "If it's all the same to you, Sheriff," he said, "I'd as soon wait till we find his car. There's enough men looking for it now. They're pretty sure to find it soon and then we could start with the dogs fresh. They're pretty beat from last night."

Masters considered this for a moment. "I think you're right," he said finally. "I'll get these boys to looking for the car."

He stepped into the center of the road and made wide, circling motions with his arms. The men from the motorcade that had followed him here had gathered nearby, waiting for instructions. Now they came closer, eyeing the dogs curiously.

"You men," Masters said. "Carter's car is hidden near here somewhere. We want to find it and use it as a starting point for the dogs. You scatter out now. Make a line of men, say ten feet apart, and start looking through the barrens clear up to the edge of the swamp. If you find the car—it's an old Buick, as most of you know by now—fire two shots, right together. I don't want any other shots for any reason outside of self-defense. Not at 'gators, not at deer. You can start now."

They began milling, taking position with a minimum of talk, the old-timers quietly taking charge. On the other sides of the swamp Masters knew that Morgan and Stifler, Combs, Bates, Ewart and Morris would have similar lines of men beating the pine barrens. If they found the car the dogs would be given the scent. If they didn't, the lines would be combed across the swamp itself. Last night's search had been hurried, a chance effort at catching a panic-driven man. Now the time had come for a systematic, unrelenting search.

There was little to be done now. Masters crouched in the thin shade cast by his car, squatting on his haunches. Young Stewart took the same position, keeping one tanned hand on the massive head of one of the dogs. Sergeant Schuster tried the position briefly and then straightened, red-faced.

"Damn tight breeches," he explained. Stewart grinned.

Charlie Hess had remained standing quietly, hardly seeming to perspire in spite of the oppressive heat. Schuster had left the shortwave set in his cruiser on; they could hear the faint crackling sputter of the carrier wave and occasional laconic orders from the dispatcher. Schuster jerked a thumb at the car.

"I've got all the off-duty men from the barracks in on this thing," he said. "Every trooper that's left on the highway is looking for Carter's car in case he tried to run for it. You put an alarm out on the sheriffs' net, didn't you?"

When Masters nodded his head Schuster continued: "We've got the National Guard helicopter arranged for. He ought to be along pretty soon. So the way I figure, I don't see how he can keep away from us for very long. Particularly if we find his car."

The crackle from the cruiser radio intensified and the metallic voice said sharply, "Dispatcher to Sergeant Schuster. Come in, please."

Schuster strode to the car and picked up the microphone. "Yeah, Daly," he said. "What is it?"

"Sheriff Masters with you?" the voice wanted to know.

"Yeah. Wait a minute."

Masters had come to his feet at mention of his name. Now he took the microphone from Schuster. "Masters," he said simply.

"Got a message to relay to you from the commanding general at Fort Benning. Says he heard about what's going on here and wants to know if he can help you out with a battalion of Rangers. Says he can have them on trucks and on the way in half an hour if you can use them."

Masters said, "Tell the general thanks and we'll be glad of the additional men." He hung the microphone back on its hook, thinking that the manhunt's tremendous appeal was not limited to geographical areas. It went deeper than that, clear back to the days when the cave men banded together for defense against wild animals.

All four men looked up at the oddly oscillating drone of a helicopter. The ugly aircraft, glinting in the sun, appeared over the treetops. Swinging back and forth in pendulum strokes, it resembled one of the tremendous dragonflies that bred in the swamp.

The dispatcher came on the air again: "Dispatcher to Sheriff Masters. The helicopter pilot says he can see four men with a pair of hounds and wants to know if you're one of them. Says if you are, wave your arms."

Masters, feeling ridiculous, stepped away from the car and waved both arms. The dispatcher came on again. "Says all right, he sees you. Wants to know if you have any instructions besides look for an old blue Buick."

Masters picked up the microphone again. "Are you going to be in contact with him?" he asked.

The metallic voice said, "Yes. I've got him on another band. I'll relay anything he tells me or that you want to tell him."

Masters said, "Tell him to work this side of the swamp first. If he sees anything, have him give it to you and you get it to me through this net. Sergeant Schuster will be with the cruiser and he'll get the message to me if I've gone into the swamp myself."

At the moment that Masters again hung up the microphone the heavy, flat report of a shotgun echoed up out of the pines. A split second later another shot crashed, splintering the silence. Masters leaped for his car.

"Schuster," he ordered. "Tell that 'copter pilot to circle the area that he sees my car go into. Stewart, get those dogs into my car. Fast, man!"

Stewart clucked to the dogs, which seemed to be alert to this new excitement. One of the animals barked, a heavy, chopping, surprisingly deep sound, before it leaped into the back of Masters' car with its partner. Masters, looking around for Hess, saw that the reporter had raced to his own car and was hastily backing and filling to get turned in the direction of the shots. Masters shot the county car across the ditch in a careening turn that had Stewart hanging on to the side of the door while the dogs slid to the floor of the back seat in a tangled mass of brown hide.

Masters turned left at the first road, depending on his feel for direction to guide him. The road dipped swiftly into the pines, second growth timber that grew astonishingly thick. After a quarter mile the crown in the center of the road was scraping against the bottom of the car and the sheriff fought the wheel to get out of the ruts, straddling them at heavy cost to the paint on the fenders. Now he could make out the running figures of several men and he turned the car accordingly, completely out of the old lumber road, picking a path through the thinnest section of undergrowth.

Ahead loomed a small mountain, pyramidal in shape, with no growth on its slopes. At the foot of the mountain a dozen men had gathered with more coming up on the run. A few old and broken timbers lay about. Masters recognized the mountain for what it was, a perfect sugar cone of sawdust, left behind by the loggers years ago. Masters jumped from the car. Where a heavy thicket of wild plum had grown up he could make out the square, boxy back end of an old car. One wheel was visible, an old-fashioned, artillery-spoked wheel; that and part of an equally old-fashioned tubular steel bumper. He shouted as he went forward, "You men—keep away from that car!" They fell back reluctantly. Beside him young Stewart came up with the dogs; they were on leash and he was having a hard time holding them back. The big animals were whining and snuffling in their eagerness. Charlie Hess was not yet in sight. Having trouble getting his heavy car over the rough road, Masters supposed, and gave it no further thought.

The car could not have been seen from more than twenty feet and not at all from the air. Masters called out, "Who found it?"

A small man carrying a shotgun stepped forward. "I did, Sheriff," he said proudly. "Name's Luke Elgin. Saw the ass end of it sticking out of the brush and I let go both barrels."

Masters said, "You come with me, then," and moved in close to the hidden car. The door to the driver's seat hung partly open, revealing torn and filthy seat upholstery. The floor mat was new, of plain black rubber, bought, probably, in one of the chain auto-supply stores. The still desolation of this ruined ground, the hanging door and the air of abandonment in the very position of the car all created an eerie effect. Masters swung open the back door. The rear seat was a litter of feathers and of animal soil, of empty oil cans and car tools thrown in helter-skelter. Used as a truck by Carter, Masters thought. He said to Luke Elgin, "Tell the boys to scatter around and start looking for anything that might have been dropped here in the last day or so. Nobody uses these roads outside of hunting season. Anything fresh they find might have been dropped by Carter."

Elgin turned away importantly and Masters turned

to Stewart. "Have you got that work shoe of Carter's?" he demanded. Stewart held it up. Masters said, "Let them smell it, and then start working them."

Stewart said, "I don't have to give them another scent, Sheriff. They had it once and they never forget it." The dogs were by this time frantic. Stewart clucked to them. "Slow, boys. Easy now. Line him out now!" Both the big heads went down and the whining stopped. They were at work now and they knew it. Stewart, hauling back against the straining leashes, said, "I'm going to hold back on 'em, Sheriff. Liable to be a long haul."

Masters turned back to the car, riffling through a mass of papers in the dashboard compartment and finding nothing of importance. Behind him he heard Charlie Hess ask, "Did you find her bag yet, Ed?"

"No," he said. "They're looking around now, Charlie. Help 'em look, if you don't mind." In that moment there came a triumphant cry from one of the searchers. Masters, looking up, saw a man coming toward him holding aloft a small overnight case. He was trailed by a somewhat chagrined Luke Elgin.

"Not a spec of mildew or nothin' on it, Sheriff," the man shouted. "Just like it was brand new. Bet it ain't been laying here no time at all! Looked behind a huckleberry bush and by God, there she was."

Masters, thinking regretfully of fingerprints that would now be smudged and useless, reached for the case. It was a cheap affair made of impregnated paper with flimsy brass fittings. The case was locked. Masters set the case down on its side and placed one knee in the center, gradually shifting his weight to thrust the knee down. In a moment the cheap lock sprang open. The sheriff threw back the two snaps and opened the case while the men in the party gathered close, forgetting Stewart and the bloodhounds.

The bag had been neatly packed; underthings, carefully folded, lay on top of light dresses. Their bulk had been enough to hold them secure. In the elastic-secured compartment in the lid a black patent leather pocketbook was tucked. Masters opened it. There were cigarettes—Masters glanced at the revenue stamp. North Carolina. Cosmetics, change, a handkerchief, a helter-skelter assortment of feminine hardware. There was, more importantly, a man's billfold with eighty dollars in it in tens. Under a glassine compartment was a driver's license also issued in North Carolina and bearing the name of Doris Hervey. Masters studied it.

"Age, twenty-three. Height, five one. Weight, one hundred and five. Complexion, blond." The sheriff read the words aloud softly.

Luke Elgin asked in a hushed whisper, "Belong to the girl they found this morning, Sheriff?"

Masters grunted. "The description fits, Elgin." He stood up. Knowing what it would do for Elgin, he said pompously, "I'm deputizing you, Elgin. You and the man who found this bag," he added. "I want you to take it and get on back to my office with it. Don't lose any time on the way. Turn it over to Deputy Danning and tell him I want the fingerprints inside it checked against the body that was found this morning. There's an address on the back of the driver's license. Tell Danning to get in touch with the Charlotte police and find out all he can about this girl."

Elgin, too excited to speak, merely nodded his head before he bent to pick up the case. He and the man who had found it began running toward the highway. Masters looked after them briefly, hoping they wouldn't wreck their car on the way to Clay City.

Charlie Hess said thoughtfully, "She must have been

a hitchhiker, Ed."

Masters, striding in the direction Stewart had taken, said over his shoulder, "It looks that way."

Overhead the helicopter dipped and swooped in a series of long bounds toward the swamp. Masters caught up with Stewart a hundred yards from the line where the ground actually softened into black muck and brown water. The smell of the swamp was heavy, a damp, fetid smell that was thick in his nostrils. His eyes on the dogs, Stewart said over his shoulder, "They're working good on it, Sheriff."

Masters dropped back a pace and turned to signal the man behind him to spread out. "Will they be able to stick with him when we hit moving water? He's no fool. That's where he'll head."

Stewart grinned. "I believe they could track under water if they had to. Anyway, there'll be scent in the air. They won't lose him now."

The dogs were moving forward at what was, for a man, a fast walk. They did not slow perceptibly when they left solid ground and plunged onto the quaking surface of Crying Woman. The big animals worked silently except for an occasional snuffle that sounded like a man's grunt of satisfaction. Without any warning the lead dog suddenly lifted his head and snuffled violently, pawing at his nose and then crouching while he whined. The second dog, in a matter of seconds, repeated the strange action of the first, while Stewart swore violently and despairingly. When Masters questioned him the trooper pointed at the water. In the stagnant backwash lay an iridescent ring. Where a tuft of grass protruded from the swamp the water reflected all the colors of the spectrum. Stewart said bitterly, "Gasoline. He dumped gasoline on the water and both of them got a nose full. They won't be any good for two days or more."

CHAPTER FOURTEEN

By midafternoon Masters had reorganized the manhunt to compensate for the loss of the dogs. The Ranger battalion had arrived and bivouacked at the edge of Crying Woman. Masters had withdrawn all search parties on the arrival of the troops and he had re-established a line of men that reached the width of the swamp. These men were moving slowly and steadily forward. Across from them only enough men remained to make certain of sighting Carter should he break from cover onto dry ground. He had made one trip back to his office to talk with his deputies. By telephone he contacted Rob Hansen and asked him to come out to Crying Woman.

Tom Danning had reported that Jake had been unable to find Benny Zurich. Zurich was under a comparatively light bond on Masters' charge of maintaining a public nuisance and Danning was excited. "Nobody out there knows where he went," he said. "Jake says that that King girl seems to be running things. She says he left early this morning."

Masters arranged for a pickup to be put out on Zurich but he failed to match the deputy's excitement. His purpose in picking up Zurich had admittedly been harassment and, in view of the subsequent finding of the bag near Joachim Carter's car, he no longer had a legitimate reason for assuming that Zurich might have employed the second dead girl at one time or another. Identification had already been positively established. Doris Hervey had been the name of the dead girl that the old Negro had found early in the morning. Fingerprints taken from her compact, from her license and other articles in her bag had matched with impressions taken from the dead fingers of the body that now lay in the little cement morgue. The Charlotte police had reported that the address on the license was that of a rooming house where the Hervey girl had lived for two years, during which time she had been a textile worker. Two days earlier she had given up her room with the announced intention of going to Florida. She had confided to friends that she was going to hitchhike; she was in the habit of hitchhiking. The Charlotte police had no record of her and indicated that her reputation was fair to good. No known relatives and would the Clay City police forward any additional information about her death that became available?

Sergeant Schuster summed up opinion that seemed to be general.

"He got out of the swamp last night," he conjectured. "He might have had some idea of getting to his home, maybe to kill his wife and son if he figured they informed against him. You've got plenty of reason to think he's crazy—religious crazy and especially on the subject of sex. I've met some like him. Usually they never miss a chance to see a cow or a mare getting bred. He killed his daughter because she was— loose, say, and he ran into this kid hitchhiking. All right, she's on the road. Maybe she talked a little raw or maybe he figured she was no good just because she was on the road. So he killed her and ran back into the swamps. It figures."

Tom Danning agreed. Masters, morosely drinking coffee from a soggy carton, said, "I guess. We'll know when we get him."

He and Schuster had then driven back to the headquarters of the manhunt. Rob Hansen, the big farmer from the Kingsbridge Pike, was waiting for them. He came forward to meet Masters, hat twisted in his hands. "You sent for me, Sheriff," he said.

Masters answered him, "Sunday night you saw a car down by your place. You didn't get a good look at it, you said, because it was full dark." He pointed to Joachim Carter's car, which had been driven out of the barrens and close to the highway. "Could that have been it?"

Hansen studied it carefully before he shook his head. "I'd like to say that it is, Sheriff," he said finally, "but I ain't sure. I don't think you want a guess. I'll say this much. It could have been the car."

Masters suspected that the farmer was feeling guilty because of his illicit liquor selling. Out of kindness he said, "We need all the men we can find down in the swamp, Hansen. I'd be obliged if you could find the time to help out."

Hansen brightened noticeably. "Why, sure, Sheriff," he said. "I've got a shotgun in the car, so happens."

Charlie Hess, who had heard the conversation, stared after Hansen. "You still want more proof that it was Carter, Ed?"

Masters lit his pipe. "According to the laws of the State of Georgia," he said, "we've got to prove a man guilty even if he confesses to a crime. I'm just looking ahead."

Hess put down his shotgun and reached for his cigarettes. "I guess you're right," he said. The reporters from the big-city papers had arrived on the scene long since. They had formed a small press camp similar to the ones Masters had seen during the war, but Charlie Hess hadn't stayed with them. He would have supposed that the local reporter would be glad of the chance to mingle with his colleagues on the big-circulation papers. There was even a rumor that a *Life* magazine photographer was flying in to get pictures of the hunt. Charlie Hess had stuck with

Masters throughout the day and the sheriff, thinking about it, supposed that the city men had been treating him as a country cousin.

The major in command of the Ranger battalion suddenly called to Masters. "They've flushed him! They called in on the walkie talkie!"

Masters moved swiftly to the side of the major, who had a large-scale map in his hand and was marking down figures repeated to him by a sergeant wearing earphones.

The major said, more calmly now, "That would be the second platoon of B Company. Not more than a mile in and due east." He bent to the sergeant. "Tell Captain Morrissey to send out flankers and get on both sides of him and then try to close in so as to surround him. Tell him to keep his civilians back so they won't get hurt."

Masters turned and started walking toward the swamp in long strides. The army officer had handled the situation properly; he could be relied on to keep on handling it in the same manner. The game was afoot now and it had become his job to make the final move. Behind him, Charlie Hess and the rest of the press contingent floundered through the muck.

It took Masters half an hour to reach Company B's sector of the line. A lean captain came to meet him and to point to a hummock of saw grass perhaps forty feet wide and as many long, isolated in a gut of open, brackish water fifteen feet wide. "He's out there," the officer said. "Do you want us to go and get him? There isn't much bottom."

Masters said, "My job now, Captain." He held up a hand for silence, turning as he did so to face the bedraggled reporters who had caught up to him by this time. Other searchers in the swamp, scores of them, had got the message that the B Company man had sent out and they were converging on the grassy hummock so that it was ringed by armed men.

Masters called out loudly, his voice sounding strange in the hushed quiet of the swamp, "Carter. You hear me. Come on out of there."

There was no answer and the sheriff took one step forward, sinking to his knees in the slime that underlay the water. "Carter," he called, "come out of there and you won't get hurt. If you don't I'm coming after you."

There was still no answer from Carter and Masters took another step forward, this time sinking to half the depth of his thighs in the warm, brackish water. He debated drawing his gun and having it ready and decided against it. It would panic Carter still further, he told himself, and knew that this was not the real reason. In cold fact he felt the absurdity of his position. It had a sense of theatricalism which would have been heightened by a drawn gun. Further, if Carter stood up to shoot he would not have a chance to aim before a dozen guns would cut him down. He debated a warning to the posse men behind him not to shoot unless Carter flashed a gun. For some reason not quite clear to himself he decided against it.

Now he was halfway across the gut of water. He called again and again but there was no answer. He took two more strides and was beginning to climb slightly when Joachim Carter stood up. Carter's clothes were covered with slime and muck that dripped from him as he arose, both his arms extended in a supplicating gesture. His mouth was open as if he were about to cry out. If it was his intention to do so, the words died in his throat. One gun blasted from the shore. Almost simultaneously a dozen more blazed in a rolling barrage that shook Carter like an empty sheet on a clothesline, literally tossing him before he collapsed like some grotesque scarecrow.

Masters had feared this even while he admitted to himself that it would take a posse of citizens to dredge Carter from the Crying Woman. He forced his way through the muck. Carter lay on his back, his mouth open and drooling blood and saliva, his entire middle shot away. In a fury the sheriff turned to face the men on the far side of the gut.

"God damn it," he shouted, "he didn't have a gun on him! Who started that shooting?" And as he asked the question he knew that no man in that crowd would admit to it. That man and the men who had fired the other shots would surreptitiously slip the empty cases from their guns and replace them with fresh shells. To admit to the shooting would be to admit to a womanish panic. If he checked guns there would be resentment. They had, by God, gone into Crying Woman to get Joachim Carter, hadn't they? And by God, they'd gotten him, too!

Masters said wearily, "Couple of you men come over here and get him. We'll take him on out to the highway." He was thinking that it would be asking too much—far too much—of old Doc Adams to bring him in here.

There began a slow trek back out to solid ground. The army captain moved up from his men once to murmur, "Sorry that happened in there, Sheriff. None of the Rangers fired."

Masters slapped at a gnat. "I know it," he said. "I'd have recognized a heavy rifle. Those were mostly shotguns that were fired and maybe a couple of light deer guns. Your people did fine, Captain. Just fine."

He was very tired. He supposed he ought to be a little proud now. Carter was dead. Lucy Carter was avenged, if you wanted to look at it from the dime novel standpoint. And the girl—what was her name—

Doris Hervey? And it wasn't anybody's fault, actually, that Carter was dead. Take a bunch of greenhorns on a manhunt and it would happen more often than not. They'd be saying right now that the taxpayers had been saved the price of a trial. A few things to clean up now and it would be over and done with.

CHAPTER FIFTEEN

Masters arrived at his office at five-thirty in the afternoon. The press, glutted with pictures, had gone. The battalion of Rangers had loaded into their trucks and headed back to Fort Benning. The men who had gathered for the hunt had dispersed except for a number who would stay late in the bars, hashing and rehashing the story of the hunt for and death of Joachim Carter. He saw Bob Dunn's trailer parked in front of the courthouse and the Bureau of Investigation man was waiting for him when he walked tiredly into his office.

Dunn grinned. "Did you leave any mud out in the swamp? I'd say you had about a yard and a half on yourself."

Masters shucked off his filthy jacket and flung it into the closet. He wanted a bath, now, and a big dinner. The bath would take care of the mud. Thinking about it, he decided that the bottle of 'shine in his desk drawer would help the sour taste in his mouth. It might erase the sense of discouragement that rode his shoulders and that he couldn't justify other than in his failure to find Joachim Carter on the previous night and the consequent death of Doris Hervey.

He reached for the bottle and offered it to Dunn, who refused it, and to Jake Bowen and Tom Danning, who silently indicated that he was to go first. When he had swallowed his drink he leaned back in his chair, hands interlocked behind his head. He spoke to Jake Bowen. "What about Benny Zurich? Did you locate him yet?" He asked the question, not caring much about the answer.

Bowen replaced the bottle on the desk. "He came back an hour ago. He'd been in Atlanta. I checked it and he'd been there without any doubt. Funny thing, Ed. That King girl knew it and yet she swore up and down to me this morning that she didn't know where he went. Almost as if she was trying to get him in trouble."

Masters said dryly, "She probably was. She'll own that place in another six months if Benny doesn't get his eyes open." He turned to Dunn. "I'm sort of surprised to see you here. You had to testify in court today, didn't you?"

Dunn answered, "You don't know what a big thing they made over the manhunt you ran today. We were getting news broadcasts on it every half hour. Even the judge kept calling recesses to listen on the radio in his chambers. You're famous, Ed. This week, anyway. He adjourned court early and I decided to come on down and see the excitement." He winked. "I had a legitimate reason to burn Georgia gasoline. I owed you a report on that handkerchief of Carter's. You still want to bother with it?"

Masters reached for a pad of paper. "Might as well. What was it?"

Dunn said sheepishly, "I haven't done it yet, Ed. I was too much in a hurry to get here. I've got the handkerchief in the trailer. It won't take half an hour to run it if you still want it."

Masters said, "Please," and stood up. He began to pace the floor as Dunn left the room with Jake casually following him. He was still uneasy and now he realized that he had been wrestling with the conviction that he had been pushed too hard in the last twenty-four hours to do any constructive thinking. On the face of it there had been no need for thought. Joachim Carter had run and he had caught him.

Tom Danning, watching him, said curiously, "What's on your mind, Ed?"

Masters stopped pacing and sat down again. "I don't know, Tom." After a moment he asked, "Read the Bible much?"

Danning shook his head. "Not in the last fifteen years."

Masters drummed on the desk top with his fingers. "Something doesn't fit and I can't put my finger on it. You remember how we found the Carter girl?"

Danning said, "Sure. Dead."

"And damn near naked," Masters said impatiently. "All she had on was her underclothing. I'm no authority on the Bible but there was something in the Old Testament about Abraham's son looking upon his father's nakedness and being punished for it—or maybe it wasn't Abraham. The point I'm making is this: Carter's kind of religion was the eye-for-an-eye, tooth-for-a-tooth school. Old Testament. The way we see it he killed two women, one of them his daughter, because they were bad women according to his standards. Can you see him taking his daughter's dress off? According to the way we have him figured, looking at a naked or near-naked woman is probably the last thing he would do."

Danning said doubtfully, "Unless he also figured that exposing her body was a—what do you call it? Symbol?"

Masters shrugged. "That might be it, I suppose. Except that he stopped with the dress. And in the case of the Hervey girl, he didn't follow his pattern."

Danning said, "He might have got scared off. What the hell, Ed, he ran when that trooper tried to arrest him, didn't he?"

"He did. He did just that." The sheriff strode from the room.

Bob Dunn was bent over a rack containing several test tubes, with Jake Bowen watching him in fascination. There was a tight frown on Dunn's face. He looked up to see Masters entering the trailer and he shook his head in puzzlement before he turned again to the test tubes. He turned, after perhaps another minute, and held both hands out in a defeated gesture.

"I checked twice, Ed," he said worriedly. "The girl's blood was A. The blood on the handkerchief is B."

Masters asked quietly, "Any chance of error?"

Dunn shook his head. "No chance. The test is simple and it's also infallible. The blood on the handkerchief did not come from Lucy Carter."

Masters said, "Then we'd better start hoping that it came from the old man himself."

Bowen said carefully, "Sure it did, Ed. It must have. Farmers are always cutting themselves. Besides, Jesus Christ, he ran didn't he?"

Masters said to Dunn, "Get what stuff you need for the test together and we'll go out to the morgue in my car and find out. It will be faster than pulling the trailer."

Bowen went with them to the morgue. Masters drove and Dunn sat in the rear seat and none of the men spoke.

Joachim Carter's body had been placed in a refrigerated drawer. The attendant, Billy, rolled the drawer from the wall and started to lift the body to the table. Dunn stopped him.

"Don't bother with that," he said. "I can get what I

want without removing it." He bent and took a blood sample with a small syringe and turned away.

Masters watched him impatiently. All the old doubts were stirred up again and he remembered a snatch of the conversation he had had with Joachim Carter and his family on Monday: "Torment? Time she did torment you, Joachim." And another conversation on the day of the funeral. Was it possible that it was only yesterday? That one had gone: "I want him to die like he killed my daughter." Masters could recall the scene vividly; could recall Mrs. Carter sitting stiffly in Martha Lafferty's best room with her gloved hands clenched in her lap. Watching Dunn now, he could almost predict what the result of the analysis was going to be.

Dunn turned around, his shoulders slumped. Masters asked with scarcely any inflection, "A-type?"

Dunn nodded. "A-type. The blood on the handkerchief, which was B-type, didn't come from Lucy Carter or," he gestured toward the drawer that held the body of Lucy's father, "him."

Masters said grimly, "Then I'm pretty sure I know where it did come from." He turned on his heel. "Come along," he said. "Bring that stuff with you. I don't think we'll need it but bring it anyway." He added, "Jake, we'll drop you off at the office. You arrange with Tom for meals and shifts. I want one of you there from now on until I tell you different."

When they had dropped the deputy off, Masters headed the car toward the outskirts of town. Dunn asked, when they had raced beyond the scattered filling stations and motels on the approaches to Clay City, "Where are we going, Ed?"

Masters, his eyes fixed on the road ahead, said shortly, "Where I went Monday. Simontown. I want to know why the Carter woman lied to me about that handkerchief."

Sam Byrd was not in his office in the courthouse. They found him in the lobby of the one movie house. The old sheriff was about to buy a ticket; when he saw Masters' expression he picked his money up and pushed the ticket back and came striding toward Masters.

"I got your message about Carter," he said. "I told his woman about it. She took it good."

Masters said evenly, "She should have," and explained to Byrd their findings on the bloodstained bandanna. When Masters had finished Byrd sucked in his breath through his mustache.

"Looks like she deliberately framed old Joachim," he said. "Still and all, she might have told the truth about finding the handkerchief where she said she did. Joachim could have got it bloodied some other way."

Masters shook his head. "Sheep blood or chicken blood, maybe. I don't see how it could have been human blood. You try to think of a situation that would account for it."

Byrd said after a moment's thought, "Guess it would take some explaining at that, Ed. You want to go out there now?"

"I do."

By the time they turned off the highway onto the red clay road leading to Carter's farm it was almost completely dark. Only a lemon-colored afterglow lingered in the sky westward and Masters had already turned on his headlights. The long yellow beams reached out in front of the car, dancing over the hollows in the rutted road and disclosing an occasional rabbit. Masters drove close to the house and the three men got out.

Masters made no attempt to conceal his purpose.

Abel Carter came to the door at their knock and to
Masters' question answered, "Ma? She's in the
kitchen."

There was a glow of lamplight toward the rear of
the house. Masters, using it as a guide, shouldered
Abel aside and walked through the damp-smelling
hall and into the kitchen. Mrs. Carter was seated at
the kitchen table, her hands neatly folded in her lap.
She glanced up and said, "Why, 'evening, Sheriff
Masters!" in some surprise.

Masters took two steps into the room so that he was
standing directly beside her. "Mrs. Carter," he said, "I
want to see your hands."

Her eyes narrowed briefly. "I don't see what for," she
said then. "Seems to me you ain't got any right telling
people what to do outside of your own county."

Sam Byrd and Bob Dunn had by this time come
into the room. Sam Byrd had a faintly mystified look
on his face but he said sternly, "I've got that right,
Mrs. Carter. You hold your hands out where we can
see them."

She hesitated only momentarily and then laughed
shortly. "I guess it can't hurt none. What's done is done."
With the words she took her hands from her lap and
spread them on the table, palms down in the yellow
lamplight. When she slowly turned them so that the
palms were up Masters could see the ugly red-brown
scab of a deep gash on the ball of her left thumb.

Masters said, "You needed a lot of blood to soak that
handkerchief of your husband's. Took a lot of nerve to
deliberately make a gash like that."

She answered almost lightly, "Could 'a done it peeling
potatoes."

He nodded his head toward Dunn. "That man can
do things with chemicals and microscopes that you
can't understand. He can tell me if the blood on the

bandanna is the same kind as yours. He's already told me that it isn't the same kind as your husband's or your daughter's. I can tell you something too. You wore gloves yesterday at your daughter's funeral. You didn't even take them off when you sat in Mrs. Lafferty's parlor."

She looked down at the scar on her thumb and slowly looked up again. "He," she nodded her head toward Dunn, "says that Lucy's blood was the same as her father's?"

Masters nodded his head, letting her make up her own mind.

She continued absently, "Wouldn't have thought that. Would have thought it was the same as mine. You're right about the gloves, Sheriff. It was pretty smart of you to figure it out. If I'd 'a taken them off you would have seen the fresh cut. Am I going to jail?" She added quickly, "I don't care if I am, though. He the same as killed Lucy."

Masters, furious at the thought that he had set Joachim Carter up as a clay pigeon, had given little thought to the legal aspect of the Carter woman's guilt. Thinking about it now, he came to the obvious conclusion that little could be done to punish this woman. The only charge that he could think of offhand would be conspiracy. If such a charge were made she would be tried before a jury of her neighbors unless he, Masters, sought a change of venue. He doubted if a jury in the entire state of Georgia would consider any punishment more drastic than a reprimand. Further, from what he had seen and heard of Carter, he could not blame her too deeply for what she had done. He said angrily, "You aren't going to jail as far as I'm concerned, Mrs. Carter. You're going to have it on your conscience the rest of your life, though, that you were responsible for his death."

She smiled secretively. "I'm going to try to bear it, Sheriff."

Masters turned to Sam Byrd. "I'm not going to make any charges, Sam," he said, saying it loud to be certain that Abel Carter heard the comment. The youth had not taken a chair. He was standing in the hall entrance to the kitchen. Masters turned toward him.

"You heard what I told Sheriff Byrd," he said. "I'm not trying to trick you. You people have caused a death; you have made more trouble for me than you realize. I want you to tell me how much of what you told me in Clay City was the truth. You owe it to me. Begin with a week ago Monday. You said your father was away most of the night on that date—right after he must have received the letter from your sister."

Abel Carter turned toward his mother. She gave no sign, made no comment, and he answered slowly, "It wasn't no lie. Pa was away like I said. And he was away the night she was killed."

"Did he use nearly a tank full of gas the way you claimed?"

The youth shook his head. "There ain't no way of knowing. The gauge ain't worked since I can remember. I made that up to make it look bad for Pa."

Mrs. Carter said, "You may as well know, Sheriff. It weren't nothin' special when he didn't come home till long after midnight. He did that many a time. You know where he went?" She did not wait for an answer. "He went down along the river bank," she continued. "The young folks used to park their cars there. He took his pleasure in watchin' them and then coming home and prayin' against 'em."

Masters reached for his pipe, calmer now; the rage was gone from him. "You said that on the night Lucy left home he beat her with a harness strap. You said that he carried on about whoremongers and fornicators even while he was beating her. There isn't any way I can put this to you gently, Mrs. Carter. Did he accuse her in so many words of—"

The Carter woman interrupted him. "Don't mind," she said. She stood up to face him. "What Lucy done I blame her for, some ways. But I forgave her. There wasn't no forgive in Joachim's Bible. He found her with the young feller I told you about. He out and out accused her while he was hittin' her. And she didn't deny it."

"Did you ever see her with the young man?"

She shook her head. "Never set eyes on him. Now, if you've finished with me, Sheriff, I'd like to get to my bed."

Sam Byrd, when they were in the car again, headed for the highway, swore. "Damn if I ever saw anything like that," he said. He wiped his forehead. "Don't want to see nothin' like it again, either. What do you think, Ed?"

Masters asked quietly, "About what?"

"You think old Joachim maybe didn't kill the girl?"

"I've been too busy running around to do any thinking, Sam. Maybe that's been the trouble. Right now I think that the wrong man got shot in Crying Woman this afternoon and I blame myself for it. How many fish camps are there around here, Sam?"

"Dozen, maybe, close by. And just about every farmer takes in boarders in the season. About Carter—if he didn't do it, what did he run for?"

"He's seen mobs before. And a trooper tipped him off that we wanted him for murder. Getting back to those fish camps, tomorrow morning I want you to check as many of them as you can. I don't suppose many of them keep registers."

"What name will I be looking for, Ed?"

Masters pinched the bridge of his nose with his

forefinger and thumb. "Name of the man who's done
the damnedest job of making a fool out of me since
my father. Charlie Hess."

Bob Dunn made a startled noise. Masters continued:
"It's been there to see right along, Bob. I'll tell you
more about it after we leave Sam."

They had pulled up on the main street of Simontown.
Masters stopped the car to let Byrd get out.

"I'll call you tomorrow, Sam," Masters said. He
shoved the car into gear and headed out of town.

CHAPTER SIXTEEN

After a mile Masters pulled the car to the side of the
road and got out. "You drive it, Bob," he said. "I want
to think about this some more."

Dunn slid over behind the wheel without speaking.
A score of questions were at the tip of his tongue but
he kept the silence, respecting Masters' mood. After a
few minutes Masters spoke but it was only to say,
"Stop in at the next filling station and call Tom
Danning, Bob. I don't want to call him myself because
he'll want to ask a lot of questions I'm not ready to
answer just yet. Tell him to arrest Charlie Hess on a
charge of murder. I think he believes he's safe but I've
already made more than my share of mistakes on this
business."

When they reached Clay City, Dunn would have
headed for the courthouse but Masters stopped him.
"We'll go to my place," he said. "Let him sweat in a cell
overnight." At Martha Lafferty's house, Masters called
Danning himself and confirmed that Hess had been
picked up. Saying nothing further to Dunn, he went
to bed.

Dunn was waiting at the breakfast table when Masters appeared in the morning. He had apparently slept well, Dunn observed. Some of the lines of strain were gone from his face and his eyes were free of the brooding expression that Dunn had seen there on the previous day.

Masters sat down and poured coffee while Dunn said querulously, "I know damn near as much about this case as you do, Ed. I can't see where you're not sticking your neck out arresting a man—and a reporter at that—on the strength of what we know."

Masters grinned. "I've been feeling pretty bad about this thing," he said. "A man hates to be made a fool of. What bothered me most was the fact that he just about got me to murder Joachim for him—it was my posse that shot him. I've been thinking about that, too. I've convinced myself that Charlie himself shot first and that his shot started a chain reaction that blew Carter apart. Later on today we'll talk to some of the men that were standing near Charlie in the swamp. Maybe one of them will remember if Charlie doesn't tell us himself."

Dunn asked acidly, "You think he will?"

Masters said, "We'll see." He changed the subject and Dunn, somewhat resentful, would not bring it up again. When they had finished their meal they drove downtown and parked in front of the courthouse. Word had spread, Masters noticed. Perhaps fifty men were gathered in front of the building, among them Charlie Hess's editor. When they clamored toward him, Masters thrust them aside with a good-natured, "Later," and strode into the building.

Jake Bowen was on duty. He explained, "Tom stayed till three, Ed." He added hopefully, "You want me to bring him in now?"

Masters nodded and made a mental bet. Charlie

would take one of two attitudes. He would come in furious and demand to know what right Masters had to order his arrest, or he would come in quietly, waiting to find out what Masters knew before he crystallized his own attitude. The sheriff won his bet. Hess, looking rumpled and needing a shave, came in quietly. His face was pallid and there was wary caution in his eyes, but he spoke quietly enough.

"Hello, Ed," he said. "You know what you're doing?"

"I do. Sit down, Charlie."

When Hess had pulled a chair out and slumped down into it Masters began, "I've been thinking about this all night, Charlie. Trouble is I started thinking a lot later than I should have. I give you credit for that. The only thing I don't know right now is whether you killed two people or four. I think probably it was four."

He watched Hess closely as he spoke. There was no change of expression on the reporter's face.

"A little more than a year ago," he began, "you went fishing up Simontown way. You met a girl, a country girl. She didn't know a lot about people and you had your way with her. Her father caught you together and you left her. I'll give you credit for this much, Charlie. You couldn't have known that she was pregnant."

A muscle flickered at the corner of Hess's mouth, but he said nothing.

"The girl's father turned her out. She had her baby somewhere, some way. We'll find out about that later. She wrote home asking for help, but her father got the letter and ignored it. This girl had no education, no way of earning a living except one. So she earned it that way. And after a while she moved on to another town and went to work at a pretty sorry place but the only kind of a place that would give her a job."

"Benny's?" Jake Bowen asked.

Masters filled his pipe and lit it before answering. "Benny's," he said. "This girl, this Lucy Carter, probably didn't know where you came from, Charlie, or she would have gone to you a long time ago. Or maybe she did go to you." He paused and looked at Hess. There was a light greasing of sweat on the reporter's forehead.

He said nothing.

Masters continued: "No, I guess she didn't go to you. But one day she ran into you. Way she was brought up, I'd say she insisted that you take care of her, marry her. Up to this point I can't blame you too much. Now I start blaming you. You were engaged to be married to another girl, a girl with money and social position. You wanted both, didn't you, Charlie?"

Hess showed his teeth in what he meant to be a grin, but he didn't speak.

"You were in a pretty bad spot, Charlie," Masters continued. "You were courting one girl and trying to stall for time with another. That must have been about the time Lucy quit working at Benny's. She felt that she had a friend, a protector, and that pretty soon everything was going to be all right for her. She didn't have to be afraid of George Cox, for example. You must have worried about that. You couldn't be sure that she hadn't told Cox about you." Masters' tone became contemptuous. "That was also about the time she wrote home to her family asking if she could come and see them. I'd say that she meant to tell her mother about the baby and about you."

Hess looked up. His voice was gritty as he said, "I'd like a cigarette."

Masters nodded at Jake Bowen, and the deputy brought out his pack and offered it to the reporter. Hess lit the cigarette and again attempted a smile. "It's a hell of a story, Ed," he said. "How does it come out?"

Masters noticed that Tom Danning had come into the room at some point in the last five minutes. He had come to a halt behind Hess, not wanting to interrupt.

"She probably got pretty impatient," Masters went on, "wanting you to keep whatever promises you had made to her. From your viewpoint, there was only one solution. You had to kill her. You took her for a ride and you left her out on the Kingsbridge Pike." Masters paused in thought for a moment and then said softly, "And, by God, I think that clears up something else."

"What's that, Ed?" Dunn asked.

"That dress business," Masters said. "She was wearing a bright yellow dress when she was last seen; Tom Danning found that out. You called it—what was it—a rhodamine dye?"

Dunn nodded his head.

Masters put his pipe down carefully. "I think," he said, "you met someone while she was with you that evening, Charlie. Maybe someone waved to you at a traffic light. Maybe, with that bad gas tank of yours, you stopped for gas. Now a girl's body is found, dressed in a bright yellow dress. They wouldn't know the girl, Charlie, but they'd remember that they saw you with a girl with such a dress. You took the dress for that reason and perhaps to make it look like a sex crime."

Hess said, "That's ridiculous, Ed. You can't even prove that I knew her."

"I'll get to that. When I finish with you I'm going to have Tom and Jake check every filling station, every newsstand, every corner drugstore. They're going to ask anybody they can find if they saw you with a girl in a yellow dress last Sunday night. Somebody is going to remember," Masters said.

Hess shifted uneasily in his seat. "Sally has a yellow dress."

Masters asked, "Will she say she was with you Sunday night?"

The reporter recovered his poise. "I didn't say she was. I just want you to see how damn silly this circumstantial case you've made up really is."

Masters stood up. "Then tell me," he said. "Did you take your vacation up on the Oconee last year—near Simontown?"

Hess was silent for a moment, seemingly thinking about the implications of the question. Then he answered, "I don't think I'm going to answer that question without counsel."

Masters had anticipated this reaction. Hess was desperate and smart. He was going to make a last-ditch fight of it. Masters said, "No matter. Sheriff Byrd is checking all the fish camps right now. I doubt if you would have used a false name. You wouldn't have had any reason to."

"Suppose I was there. What would that prove?"

"Proof isn't going to be hard to get, Charlie. We were hoorawing off in the wrong direction. We never even asked if you had an alibi for Sunday night because who in his right mind would have suspected you?" Masters turned to Dunn and his voice was sharp and incisive. "Bob, the night you found the maker's label in Lucy Carter's shoe and we traced it down and found out where she came from, I told you not to mention it to anyone. No offense, but did you let it leak out?"

Dunn shook his head. "As I stand here, no," he said.

Masters wheeled on Hess. "Yet, when I came back from Simontown, you said in so many words that you 'weren't expecting me so soon.' I thought it was just an idle comment at the time. It wasn't. You knew I had a lead on her hometown, but to have known how far away it was you had to know its name, which meant you must have known Lucy herself—and you knew where it was or you couldn't have expected me at any special time."

Hess said, "I'd like another cigarette." When Bowen had given it to him he said carelessly, "That isn't much, Ed."

Masters said, "It doesn't have to be. We'll know where to look and what to look for now."

The telephone pealed, sharp in the quiet of the room. Masters picked it up. The call was unimportant but he answered it. "Yes ... yes ... I see ...." staring intently at Hess throughout the conversation. The reporter licked his lips, caught himself and compressed his mouth, his gaze fixed on the receiver until the moment that Masters hung up.

Masters made no mention of the conversation, being obvious about the omission. "I'm sick of you, Charlie. I want you out of my sight. I'll tell you why I know you killed Lucy Carter and the Hervey girl and probably George Cox and old man Carter and then you can get on back to your cell and think about it. We had a girl murdered here. Her mother and brother came to the funeral under circumstances that were more than usually tragic. You, a reporter, stayed away from it. A good reporter—and I think you are a good reporter—couldn't have been kept away with a tractor, unless he was afraid that either the mother or the brother might have seen him with the girl and might remember him."

Hess sat a little straighter. "I had another story to cover. George Cox had committed suicide, if you'll remember."

Masters shook his head. "You had cleaned that up already. And about that suicide. Two people saw the body before you did. Both asked one obvious question. Did he leave a note? You, of all people, didn't ask that question—because you knew there was no note. Lucy had told you about Cox, including the fact that he hung out at one of the cabins. You knew where to look for him. I think you killed him because you didn't know how much Lucy had told him. Any scandal would have wrecked your marriage and your job. You want more?"

"Sure. I'm not going any place, apparently."

"You referred twice to Lucy's father as the old man before you had any legitimate knowledge of what he looked like. She was young. He could have been in his early forties for all we knew." Masters noticed that Tom Danning, with a pistol in an open holster, had edged closer to Hess, and he waved him back.

"By that time," Masters continued, "we had an accusation against the old man; we had an alarm out for him. That put you in a terrible position. If we picked him up you were as good as convicted, because you would have had to interview him and he would have recognized you from Simontown. But you got a break. He was picked up, but a stupid policeman made a bad blunder and let him escape. The break for you was that he got scared and ran into the swamp. He knew what his wife and son thought of him and guessed that they had accused him and that I would believe them. When—if—he came to his senses there were men beating the swamps. He could hear them, probably see their flashlights. He knew what it was to be hated and he had good reason to believe that if he showed himself he would be shot down like an animal. We had a posse out looking for him, Charlie. In this part of the country that's just about the biggest news story there is, but you didn't cover it. You were out looking for him yourself because you felt that you had to get to him before we did. Then you saw a girl standing beside the road hitchhiking. You've seen manhunts before; you know what a mob of men will do if they're inflamed to the right pitch. You killed the girl in the same manner that you killed Lucy Carter, knowing that the old man would be blamed for both and knowing further that the second crime put him beyond the bounds of human tolerance. Because you were a reporter you were able to stay with me the next day—and I, of all people, would be informed when the pack closed in. When Carter started to surrender you pulled the trigger that fired a dozen guns."

Tom Danning said softly, "Jeeesus." Jake Bowen nudged him and said, "Ssh."

Hess stared at the floor. Without looking up, he asked, "That was Sheriff Byrd on the telephone, wasn't it?"

Masters, watching him fixedly, made no reply. He had the feeling that Charlie Hess would break now if he was going to break. Hess did not. He sighed audibly and straightened his shoulders. "I'm not going to make it easy for you, Ed," he said. "You still haven't made a case against me."

Masters reached again for his pipe. "I'll give you that much," he said, "but I've already promised you we can do it now that we'll be looking right at you. Something else. When we were examining the Hervey girl's body yesterday morning you asked if we had found her bag. Later on, when we found Carter's car you asked again if we had found her bag. A man uses one word for one thing and another word for another thing. When you asked Sally Martin to hold your billfold for you, you told her to put it in her pocketbook. How did you know, if you hadn't picked her up, that the Hervey girl was carrying a bag rather than a pocketbook? I think you realized your own slip of the tongue, Charlie, but you reasoned that it would be safer to try and brazen it out than correct yourself. And when Luke Elgin found Carter's car you followed me in your car but you were late showing up. Because you were planting that bag, I'm pretty sure."

Hess seemed to have withdrawn into himself. His face was impassive.

Masters stood up again. "I'd say you were pretty lucky to have come so close to getting away with it, Charlie. I had a weakness that helped you. I wanted to see Benny Zurich guilty. I wanted to believe that it was George Cox when it began to look as if it couldn't be Zurich. And I was too damn ready to accept an accusation against Carter because, in his own way, he was a monster. You were lucky he didn't see you before all this began."

"When do you mean?" Hess asked.

"When he was in Clay City a week before his daughter was murdered. He had a letter, Charlie, remember? She wrote home and lied a little about how well she was doing. The old man drove down to see for himself. He only needed to see where she lived to draw his own conclusions."

Masters strode toward the window. "That's pretty much the way it happened, isn't it, Charlie?" He had held up the whole ugly picture for the reporter's inspection, hoping to shock some admissions out of the man. But Hess had been tough. No matter. The end result would be the same. Over his shoulder Masters said, "Ah, take him away, Jake."

He heard the scrape and scuffle as chairs were shoved back and a shuffle of moving feet. They paused, and Charlie Hess said, "See you, Ed."

Masters, looking out of the window, did not turn around. The grass in the little park below the window was already turning brown. It was going to be a hot summer.

THE END

Harold Robert Daniels was born November 3, 1919, in Winchendon, Massachusetts. He graduated from college in Milford, Connecticut, and became a specialist in the metal industry. He was editor of *Metalworking* magazine from 1958 to 1972. In the 1950s he began publishing short stories, and in 1955 he published his first novel, *In His Blood*, which was nominated that year for an Edgar for Best First Novel. John D. MacDonald praised his fourth novel, *The Snatch*, as "one of the modern classics of crime and punishment." Daniels' last novel and first hardback original, *The House on Greenapple Road*, was published by Random House in 1966. He died October 1, 1980 in Washington D. C.

Made in the USA
Columbia, SC
11 February 2023

11655050R00107